C000135806

KING DAVID

KING OF THE STREETS

Bobby Montague

Copyright © 2023 Bobby Montague

All rights reserved

The characters and events portrayed in this book are fictitious. Any similarity
to real persons, living or dead, is coincidental and not intended by the author.

No part of this book may be reproduced, or stored in a retrieval
system, or transmitted in any form or by any means, electronic,
mechanical, photocopying, recording, or otherwise, without
express written permission of the publisher.

I would like to thank my Mom for always reading to me as a kid and giving me the desire to read more and to write thanks to my dad for my determination .

CONTENTS

INTRODUCTION

David King ruler of the streets thought long and hard about how he would exact revenge on those that crossed him now came the moment of truth he was a free man once again.

Bobby Montague
PO Box 472373 Aurora co,80047

KING DAVID

BY Bobby Montague

Chapter 1: The Reversal

D avid King was pacing back and forth in his cell thinking about the last 5 years of his life that he had spent locked behind prison walls. He couldn't believe he had been off the streets that long ever since he was set up. His lawyer had finally come through on his promise to get his sentence overturned on appeal. King had enough of the starchy food that tasted like it was intentionally made to punish prisoners, and the brutal prison guards who thought that beating inmates was a sport. Once an inmate had been beaten so badly the pupils of his eyes were permanently damaged, so badly that he could barely see anything, he was eventually declared legally blind and when he eventually went home, he would never speak about how he went blind. David was also tired of the feds coming day in and day out month after month trying to scare him into believing that instead of the state prison, he was in they had a federal cell awaiting him when and if he ever got out since he refused to help them in any cases. King had missed his girlfriend Destiny who had stuck with him during his 5-year bid at Jackson correctional facility in Jacksonville Florida. He also hoped that she remained faithful because if she did, he planned on marrying her. King had made a lot of mistakes in their relationship and upon his release he planned on spoiling her he love Destiny and wanted to show her how much she meant to him by being faithful and

making things up to her no matter how long it took. It was about 830am when they called his name. He started packing all his belongings including his mail, court documents and some personal items. He would not missed being confined in the rusty old cell that reeked of must and body odor and would never missed the screams of the men that suffered from long sentences there were rapes of men from other men that was rampant in the prison. He wouldn't miss the harsh violence he had seen through his incarceration. On his first day David saw a man stab another inmate across his throat the blade went so deep that it came out the other side of the man's neck dripping crimson blood as the man fell to the dirty hard concrete floor having a seizure until he died with a hole the size of a golf ball in his neck. The smell was horrible. It was worse than the smelly often flooded toilet in his cell that always smelled like feces and urine. There were writings on the wall from years of inmates in and out of the revolving door of the system. David told himself he would never be back but the truth is only time would tell. His lawyer was good but warned him that the state was mad and already had been working with the feds to keep an eye on him. Ryan Bock the best criminal lawyer money could buy was the best at raising doubt in the minds of any juror he had been in law over 20 years he was 56 years old and dressed the part nice Italian suits with a menacing bald head and trimmed goatee he had hundreds of wins 300 to be exact with only 1 lost and that lost came from a man who paid him to lose so he could go to prison because the cartel told him to. David thought about his future, his family and his crew. And threw all the time he did he never thought about giving up the streets until this very moment. The guard called David's name and prison i.d. number and when he did that broke him out of his trance. He went through brutal times with the guards beating him whenever they felt the need to for no reason other than sport. The other inmates were also beaten. Anytime they claimed or said anything they would be more brutal to the inmates to show them who's in charge and who's running things and because they felt inmates were nothing but animals and David was no more than a washed up drug kingpin that would never get out anyway. David walked down the tier moments from freedom smiling to himself and thinking, I showed them all, now I'm getting out and who's the loser now. He was always told to hire the best lawyer money could buy because you will for sure need him one day if you are committing crimes. It was the right thing to do and now he was about to go free. David, do you hear me calling you ? an inmate named Just said David looked up, still smiling. What's up Just? I didn't hear you. I was daydreaming, well snap out of it. I hope you weren't leaving without saying goodbye to your comrade? "No way" Just you're my friend and you helped me when I first arrived at this hell hole and you never switched up on me and for that you have my loyalty forever. I learned everything about this place from you. I couldn't have survived it without your input. I have plans for you old buddy but for now I'm going to send you 1500 a month so you can be comfortable with the little time you have left. Hell you will be getting out soon also. Yeah David I get out in 18 months but you don't have to give me anything, you good people. You are a strong minded young buck but you have learned discipline and self control during your time here. All I wanted from you and all the young guys was to be safe and to know prison is not a joke. I wish I had an older inmate or anyone to teach me the ropes when I first got here then maybe I wouldn't have done these 20 years in the belly of the beast. That's all water under the bridge now or is it under the dam? I forget which. I'm getting out soon either way but fuck all that you're getting out now and as you promised I will have a job in your organization.   Inmate 91792 you have 15 min until release said the burly guard David yelled back ok I'm on the way I'm almost ready. The guard shot back you better be count is over and you don't have a choice unless you want some more ass whippings before you leave. David looked at the guard and made a mental note that if he ever saw him on the street he would punish his bitch ass. As you can tell, I will not miss this place. Well go ahead, get out of here. David started to walk off as Just sat back down on the cold steel chair in his cell. Just recalled when he first met David he was a well built 20 year old young man full of courage and stubborn as a bull. Just could tell David never been locked up before in his life by the naive expression on his face he decided to take the young man under his wing and teach him the ends and outs of prison life because with a 20 year sentence he would have to learn about the drugs being brought in and how not to indulge in them if he didn't want to get caught up in gang wars. But also told him if he insisted on the hustle he showed him how to push it through the prison but thankfully David never got caught up in those rackets. He told him how to make wine which the prisoners called hooch, also which guards were dirty and who he could bribe so he could get practically anything in and out of the system. Just had warned David it was best to stay clear of all those things and he was glad David had taken his advice because once you started there was no way out but death. The prisoners lived by the code blood in blood out. David stayed clear and kept working on his appeal and it paid off he was a free man. Justin Clark inmate 57911 was sentenced to 23 years and had done 20 on the sentence was scheduled to be released in 18 months. Just though back to the day he entered the Jacksonville correctional facility in Jacksonville Florida. he was a scraggly 20 year old 5 ft 7 158 pound black man that just had been handed down a lengthy sentence. His charges were first degree murder and arson. He took a plea for 23 years to avoid serving fed time for the arson. The truth of the matter Just didn't care because he did so many other killings that they never found out about and so much dirt he did so he felt 23 years was lite time compared to all the major crimes he committed besides he was only locked up because he didn't leave the scene of the crime fast enough he lingered around torturing the victim. When the police showed up he was so into killing the man, he was having so much enjoyment he didn't want to run. The victim was known as Kevin Spade aka Ace of Spades, leader of the Black Spades, the most violent gang in the state of Florida. Just as the gang's plug he fronted Kevin a kilo in which he never repaid Just and never responded to Just Phone calls and Just took that as a sign of disrespect especially since they had been in business for years. Kevin had finally sent word to just that he wasn't paying and they could handle it in the streets which Just knew he couldn't let slide or the streets would see him as weak and then pounce on him so he decided to teach Kevin and the Black Spades a lesson. Little did they know how crazy Just is. This is the same man years prior he put a baby in a microwave for 20 min because the baby father owed him 20 dollars so he figured killing the child would make them even, hence the name Just meant he would do just about anything to get revenge on anyone who crossed him. Just found out where Kevin lived thru his contacts in the streets and waited on the perfect opportunity then broke in the house by cutting off the alarm, something he learned how to do in boys group homes as a teen. He cut the main wire switch then put foil between the receptor and the house and the alarm went off. He went in thru the front door by picking the lock since he didn't have to worry about the alarm anymore and waited until Kevin came home. The more Just waited the more angrier he became at the man the streets call Ace of spades how dare this bitch ass nigga try me and test my gangsta he's a joke and I'm going to discipline him for good with torture and making a laughing stock out of me in the street as he thought of all the things he would do the key turned in the master cylinder of the front porch lock. Kevin came thru the door baby I'm home Spade called out to no one in particular he laughed out loud because he loved saying this being a single man. Just made his move the first shot hit Kevin in the left knee cap shattering his bones. Kevin stumbled, The second shot hit him in the right leg crushing an artery which left the leg dead and spun him around the force was so blunt he knocked a lamp off the end table, The third shot hit him in the spinal cord he fell face first his body dropped like a sack of potatoes, unable to feel anything from below the waist he had no idea of what was going on but he was deftly afraid. Just walked up and stood towering over Kevin, his 5 ft 7 inch 158 pound frame looking more like a 6 ft 4 man spun Kevin around to face his judgment day. Kevin looked in Just eyes and knew he was going to die a horrible death and that he underestimated the man in front of him. Hello Kevin a menacing looking Just said you wanted me to handle it in the streets so here i am you bitch ass nigga, I'm going to enjoy hearing you scream and after i kill you i will find any family you have and kill them to i will start with your mother by torturing her and keeping her alive for years until i get tired. please!! please!! Just I'm sorry i have the money in the bedroom in my safe. Just reached down and smacked the shit outta Kevin with his German luger pistol no need to beg Ace of Spade. Just said sarcastically as he spit mucus out his mouth that fell on Kevin face and dripped down his lip causing Kevin to cry, please!! I can't feel my legs. I will do anything I can pay you double please don't touch my mom please let me live. Just! say something i was joking , I didn't mean the things i said please Just! Just! Answer me. Just calmly placed duck tape on Kevin's mouth so he couldn't scream anymore and he stood there laughing enjoying the moment. He slapped Kevin in the mouth to wake him up because he was in and out of consciousness. You wanted to be a tough guy he said then immediately he stabbed him in both palms of his hands leaving the butcher knives protruding through his bleeding flesh lodge to the floor underneath causing Kevin to squirm. Just took his dick out and humiliated him more by pissing in his face drink up lil bitch he said as the warm salty piss filled up Kevin's mouth eyes and face causing him to throw up in his mouth. Just cared nothing about D.N.A. that he would be leaving behind the devil was in him and all he wanted to do was humiliate his prey. Without warning he stood over him again and stabbed him in his right eye as he said the words hear no evil see no evil you tough mother fucker Kevin spassed out in pain he never felt before in his life praying that he would just kill him already. He was trying to scream through the duct tape so Just ripped it off Just! You better leave another alarm going off if the first one doesn't the police will be here in any minute. Just look down at Kevin without warning and stomped him in the face causing his nose to go backwards into his face making him look deformed shut the fuck up its too late for all that fuck the police your going to feel my wrath. Just stomped on Kevin for 10 min straight breaking his ribcage in 5 places the bones were sticking out his chest like meat at the slaughterhouse. I'm going to show you how much i give a fuck about your silent alarm he reached over and grab a can of gasoline he brought with him and started pouring it all over Kevins body then he unzipped his pants and pored it down his pants I'm gonna set your dick on fire first he said looking like a devil the he sat down and took out a Dutch master cigar and crack it down the middle and filled it up with some Cali mist the weed was so strong it woke Kevin up out of his unconscious Just lit the blunt and took a few pulls as he said to Kevin I'm going to tell your mom as i fuck her in the ass you put up a fight do you have any last words. Kevin sensing the end was near manned up and said see you in hell motherfucker. Just then placed the cigarette in Kevin's open zipper hole burning his penis first like he promised. He screamed in pain as his flesh melted off his body like a pig at a BBQ on the grill. Just headed to the front door then turned around and said to Kevin's dead corpse check mate bitch. He opened the squeaky doors and headed down the stairs. When he got to the bottom he opened the door and two police officers were standing there with their Glocks pointed at Just. Freeze cock sucker officer Malone screamed. I wish you would fucking blink and i will blow your head off your body his partner officer Lomax said. You got me, officers Just said to the police who he feel had the drop on him. Turn around put your hand on top of your fucking head now. Just complied with the officers. Boom! Boom! The house burst into flames and all the windows exploded. The house was burning fast, it was bright blood red and smelled of death. The smoke could be seen for miles. Dispatch this is officer Malone and Lomax we have a signal 13 and it's getting worse the fire has just caused a big explosion and we have a suspect in custody we believe just did a 211 from all the blood on his clothes . ok officer Malone this is Jessica from dispatch an ambulance and fire truck is on the way to secure the suspect. Let's put this dirtbag in the car Lomax said and also make sure the cuffs are tight. Malone there comes the fire truck lets take this dummy to the precinct the two officers pulled off as the fire truck and homicide pulled up as they were driving they asked Just did he have anything to say Lomax said he asshole I'm sure you killed Kevin back there we been investigating him for years and you just fucked up our case we knew something was wrong when the tracker we put on him went dead in the house see if you have know that u probably wouldn't be here said Lomax. Don't talk to this black son of a bitch Lomax/ Malone said spitting racial slurs at Just. Officers, I would like to use my 5th amendment rights to remain silent. They remained silent until they pulled up to the 85th precinct; the building was a known corrupt hell hole. The feds had been trying to catch Malone and Lomax for years along with all of their corrupt colleges but the attempts had been futile. Which interrogation room are you taking the suspect to? Detective Johansson asked. Room 2 responded to Lomax. Mr. Justin Clark I'm detective Johansson you have the right to remain silent you have the right to request an attorney and you have the right to stop this interview at anytime do you understand these rights as i have explained them to you yes replied Just ok I'm going to get right to it Justin Clark we found the body we found your fingerprints and D.N.A. Officers Malone and Lomax got you coming out the front door of the house we have you dead to rights i would like to close this case up so sign this confession so we can both get up outta here I can go home and you can go to jail do you have anything you want to add or say. All I want is my lawyer responded Just look here Mr. Clark, this is. Fuck the police locked me up officer i have nothing to say pig. Ok tough guy when you get you will be an old man. Fuck you Just shot back I'm only 20 I will be fine when i touched back down and i am tough and when i get the fuck out i still will be the same tough guy no matter how long it takes. Ok so be it Johansson said lets go to your cell. Just wasted no time instead of life with no parole his lawyer got him 23 years he signed the plea agreement and went off to prison. Its been a long journey Just thought to him self now I'm going to sit back and do this small time left and relax no more anything i will be working out getting myself ready for the free world and David will give me work when i get out I'm going to take back over all my shit anyone not down with me will get rolled over you either with me or against me and i don't give a fuck who you are get ready world, Justin Clark is back real soon. I need to start planning my take over of the city again by getting me a gun connect and a drug connect which i believe David will do fine long as he can supply what i need i also need to make sure anything or anyone that has a problem with what i did to the king of spades is eliminated so i don't have issues later on after i take care of those then i can stack my money up and find a lil nigga in the progress to run my shit because I'm going to semi retire on an island far from the extradition of the united states and have my lil man work for me and he can take the heat from law enforcement while i pull the strings and be the kingpin i was destined to be I'm gonna give the state and the city a run for the money it will be epic nothing like they have ever seen before.

CHAPTER 2: FREE AT LAST

Finally free after 5 years now where my woman said she was going to be out here in a black on black Audi all i see is correction officers cars. David! David! Over here oh shit there she is come here give your man a kiss david put me down im up to high in the air you only been home 5 min and already you got me screaming your name, and you sound so good screaming it i thought you said you would be in an audi but i'm not mad this maserati truck is hard as hell this is something i would drive. The truck is for you. You can go to the motor vehicle when you get a chance. You're not on any papers so if the police stop you it will only be a ticket .Destiny chill out with the police talk. Let's get outta here i'm driving. Damn this car is fast as hell baby the peanut butter interior is tight i love it thanks babe. I knew you would be where you wanted to go first. Let's drive through the city and let me enjoy my first day home with the woman I love.I love you to baby. Hey destiny, let's get some food before we start the 4 hour trip back home to miami. Ok babe what about that seafood spot right there on hood landing road ok babe pulling over now. Thanks babe I see you haven't lost your gentleman touch you opened the door for me to the car and pulled my chair out at the table, from now on only the best treatment for you baby you stayed loyal and held me down at least as far as i can tell. Far as you can tell oh you got jokes this pussy hasnt been entered in 5 years you probably gonna nut as soon as i put it on you if i put it on you. Ok babe you win i'm waving the white flag lets order i'm starving where is the server excuse me sir i'm your waiter Saul may i get you and your date some drinks and start off with any appetizers yes let me get a matter fact where is my manners the lady would like if my memory serves me correct chicken baked macaroni and a pasta salad am i right babe yes david it's still my favorite dish oh and may i have a glass of white wine any brand will do yes miss and sir what will you have the pleasure of having well since this is the first dish i've ate in a restaurant in awhile i would like the porterhouse t-bone with wild rice and a baked potato and a sweet tea with light ice please . Ok your dishes will be ready in 15 min. Hey baby you know the whole time i was in there i was thinking of all the times i came home late of all the times i took your love for granted and i can promise you right now that will never happen again i see you was really down for your man you came to visit you put money on my books and anything i asked you did and for that i'm going to be forever grateful to you . That place breaks people and I stayed strong with your love and the letters and visits. I also met a brother named Just that I'm gonna look out for when he gets out but I don't wanna say anything more because I don't like to involve you in my business. David i here you and i believe you i also know your going to pick off where u left off but in order for me to endure this i need some reassurance that there is an out plan i don't want to go thru this again and i know you were set up with the guns and drugs in your car but next time if there is a next time it could be worse or better yet death. Baby Destiny look i can promise you this . excuse me sir you fool is arriving. Thanks Saul now baby like I was saying I can promise you this after I get the person or people responsible for setting me up and I figure out who's going to run my day to day operations. I'm going to retire and run some real estate and some other business ventures. yeah i hear you David but that not out for good there still will be risk. Babe everything in life is risk i will be what they call the money man i wont be near anything i will be so insulated from the life that feds or any police won't be able to connect me to anything even if they expect it so don't worry i got this just trust me on this but anyway let's change the subject for now isn't this food awesome yes david they really did a good job i'm almost done . Waiter excuse me, waiter may I have the check please yes sir here is your bill thanks hold up here is 200 dollars sir it's only 125 dollars keep the change come on baby lets go. Ok we're on the turnpike going thru i95 south will be there in 4 hours maybe 3 in this truck you looking real good baby and i missed you so much

David you have plenty of time to show me how much you miss me. While i was gone did my crew drop the money off at the spot on time every month yeah they did your crew i will give it to them they are loyal and that's rare yeah i know i hand picked them all myself they some stand up guys but there is no one in the group that i consider a leader that can run it all in my absence. Oh, we're here now. Finally I miss our home north coconut grove. It's my palace. I missed it but not much as i missed you lets go in grrr ruff ruff grrr is that dollar barking stop that shit boy it's me your owner come here. Oh shit this dog got big as hell he knocked me down. I will have to spend some time with him so he can get back to me. Forget the dog david let's go now bedroom dam girl you ready lets go good night dollar. Damn baby you really miss me. We've been lovemaking for hours and you came twice yes Destiny and you came hundreds of times ok mister don't toot your own horn you put it down i give you that now i'm going to sleep I'm tired . me to good night babe i love you . I love you baby. Good morning babe I'm showered. I have to go talk to my guys today. I will see you later ok alright i will probably go shopping myself see you later give me kisses ok i'm taking the truck i love it see ya later. Wow my mans finally home. I remember when I first met him at the mall he smelled so good, Paris Hilton for men was the scent and his conversation was awesome. Never judged me on my past with my family. David was 6ft 200 pounds pure muscle he worked out 3 days a week and kept his hair in 8 rows of cornrows. It was love at first sight and he never judged her about her past. Destiny Rainey father Ishmell Rainey and mother Aisha Rainey were the bonnie and clyde to the streets they lived fast and died hard they had Destiny when they were both 18 years of age Ishmael was a stick up kid that gradually moved to robbing banks he met Aisha when he robbed all her friends one day with no mask on and she saw him at a corner about to get in a jitney van one and went off on him but he quickly turned the tables on her and charmed her he even gave her all the things he took from her friends for her to give them back and that is something stick up kids don't do never do they give items back but he was so smitten with the chocolate skin beauty with the flawless body and a ass so big you could lean on he had to have her and before long they were inseparable it wasn't long after Aisha was curious on how much money he made and could it maintain both of them so he started to explain to her the game of robbing and it turned her on so she suggested she go with him now from the begging he was not with it but after her very persuasive ways and her giving him everything he wanted in the bed room he was sprung so he agreed the regular robbing drug dealers got tired so they started hitting banks they go in and was out in 120 seconds after robbing 10 banks and only sitting on 200 thousands they decided they needed to stop the banks because they were hot so they came up with a plan to rob one of the biggest drug dealers in atlanta named Crazy Eddie who was known to kill off whole families and had contacts in the police force and the feds. They had been scoping him out for months and found out he went to the mosque to pray by himself because he thought he was safe but little did they know he was so keen on game he knew someone was following him and he had his men sitting everywhere so when they tried whatever they tried they would die and all there family would go to hell with them. On the day of the heist they drop their 10 year old daughter off in miami to see her grandmother then they flew back to atlanta to do the biggest heist of their life soon as they got back to atlanta they found Crazy Eddie and followed him to the mosque when he went in they waited 20 min then went in 2 guns in Aisha hands and Ishmell had the sks long barrel assault rifle from the moment they kicked in the door something was off, the mosque was empty when they knew they saw him come thru the door they searched the building and couldn't find anything Aisha had a bad feeling and wanted to leave but at the last min Ishmell found another door that was behind a curtain and they both entered when they came thru the door they smelled a funny odor which they didn't realize was a sleeping gas when they awakened they was in a chairs tied up. Do you know who the fuck i am? i'm crazy mf Eddie and you thought you were gonna rob me you stupid mother fucker i knew you two idiots were folling me from day one i have surveillance im no small time street hood stop crying bitch. Tash slap this bitch but use the hammer.(thump,thump). Now look at you bitch your skull is cracked open your leaking i can see your white meat lets see what your nigga has to say, you see i dont hit bitches that's why i let tash crack that bitch in the head now you the leader i want you to think about this while your suffering from the 2 gun shots to each leg.(bang,bang) Was it worth it was it fucking with this million dollar nigga and i know about your baby girl Destiney i did my home work on you two when i find her im gonna kill her so that way i never have to worry about no get back so where every you hid the bitch at i will find her eventually and off her lil ass. Look man i will pay you i will work for you please don't hurt my baby girl. It's too late for begging and I don't hire loser bank robber stick up kids now Tash take this sks and blow their heads off their body. Ok(boss ratt ta tat tat bang bang) hey boss what u want us to do with the bodies. Putem in front of they house that way the next motherfucker will think twice before fucking with me. Ring,ring,ring,ring The phone woke Destiney outta her daze hello whats up baby i was calling to check up on you you good yeah im ok i was thinking about my parents and that crazy guy that the streets in the Atl said killed them baby calm down he dont know where u at and if he did hes not strong enough to fuck with us if you feeling uneasy and you think anything let me know i can send my squad to kidnap his ass and you can kill him yourself to avenge you peoples murders. No babe i want to leave that alone it's not like my parents were in the right or something i just want to be left alone that all. Ok babe you got it whatever you want ok i will talk to you later. Ok later babe i love you . I love you too. Yo Ryder I may need you to kill Crazy Eddie ass outta Atlanta soon but I will let you know. Ok King let me know I'll off his ass and then we can take over Atlanta too. Ok i will but for now be easy and go distribute that work to all the workers and collect that money a.s.a.p. Ok King I'll update you later on my progress. Bet I'm about to go home, holla. Babe im home where u at im right here David what's up? Here is some money for you to go shopping with, about 10k buy you something nice you deserve . Ok babe things must be going well these last few months you've been home. Yeah shit been ok i got Ryder running the crew and giving out all the work i may have underestimated him he may be ready after all to run shit i just have to get him to see sometimes you have to be willing to work or talk things out it doesn't have to always result in violence you only need that when it's necessary but other than that he coming along real well i'm gonna go check up on the workers in a bit but afterwhile i want even do that no one will see me only Ryder and he will report to me and it's only if things are to outta his control will he even call on me so you see retirement is closer than we think. (beep,beep) This is him texting me now. Hello, what's good? Hey boss we got a lil problem here. Ok where you are, I'm at the block in Little Haiti. Say no more, I'm on the way. Ok Haitian Frank the boss man is almost here when he gets here keep that same energy you got talking gangster. Fuck you talking bout same energy blod clot im jamacian and Haitian we born with the energy them fucking bricks is too dam high 17k i should be getting them for 10k easy and if you or your boss man dont like it he can.(Knock!knock) good he's here tellem yourself. Ryder what's up king this mother fucker talking about the bricks too high and he will go elsewhere .So you called me out here for this piece of shit.(Smack) yo mon why the bumbaclot you slap me. First off im the King your king and you will address me as such i will explain this shit one time and one time only bricks for your fake jamaican haitian ass is 17k as long as you get 50 bricks when you step up to a 100 like the rest of my people then you move to 10k now if you dont like it you can give up everything and step the fuck off but let me warn you this is my block and Ryder is my second in command you leave you dont come back you go get work somewhere else but you wont go your no leader youre used to getting spoon feed like all bitches are. So with that said get yo bitch ass back to work. Ok mon take it easy it wasn't that serious i'm good Ryder just didn't explain it. Shut yo lying ass up i just told you to keep that same energy when king gets here but now you switch up. Ok Ryder check this out im trying to give you more sociable so you can call for everything it's up to you to call the shots if you felt he deserve bricks for 10k it was on you and sometimes you don't have to resort to violence you can talk to a person a certain way to get your point across. Ok King I will start to do much better. No you are doing a great job you just have to learn how to problem solve better. Anyway I have to get outta here. I have to pick up my boy. Just from prison he got out early he had eighteen more months to do but they let me out after only doing three on that because of prison overcrowding and he's at the end of his sentence anyway. Is he coming into our thing? No, I doubt it. I'm probably gonna put him on then we will supply him. He has his own thing going on in Overtown from what I understand and he got some shit outta state. So is he a stand up dude. Come on Ryder if i say he is then he is. You're gonna meet him and supply him so be easy. Ok David if you say it's so then it is what time you are going to get him. I'm about to leave now. I will holla at you later. Dam this fucking highway is crowded as fuck let me call Destiney and tell her my move real quick.(ring,ring) hello King hey babe i'm on my way to the prison actually im close to the prison picking up Just the guy that held me down i will see you later did you go shopping. Yeah I went to the mall with my girls. I bought them some things if that's ok with you . Sure listen babe when i give you something it's your to do as you please ok. Ok David i got it let me know when you're on your way home .Ok babe.(ring,ring) who the fuck number is this let me answer it may be Just. Hello, what's up? What's good King it's Just where u at. Oh shit Just im pulling up in a black on black 7 series bmw. Ok cool i see you coming down now. Dam King this car is hard as fuck this my type right here. Oh yeah i knew you say something close to that that's why i bought this for you. My nigga are you for real. Hell yeah i will drive us to the city drop myself off at my maserati and you go do your thang. Yo for real you a real nigga. What are your plans after all this time being locked up? I was telling my young worker the spot you used to have but I don't know how you are going to go about getting that back. Its simple king they get down or i run them the fuck over. Well said just you are hungry. No, I'm ready to get to work. Bro you just came home don't you want to get some pussy party or anything. Hell no, I'm hitting the ground running. I'm ready. Ok suit yourself so what's the plan. First thing im going over in overtown and telling them what it is they know me but if one of them young bucks try to jump his ass will get discipline and then im going to call in my crew the Haitain mob to clean up all niggas who not with us. Dam Just i like your style you don't play any games that's exactly how i roll you either get with the program or get run over for real. Got that shit right King. So Just how was it when you found out you were getting out 15 months sooner i know shit hit you by surprise. Well to keep it 100 with you they said thru the prison council they were going to let out 500 inmates because of overcrowding and you know the prison holds 2500 inmates but we was at 3500 so it was very overcrowded people sleeping 3 in a 2 man cell shit was crazy but when they called my number i was very surprised because my crime was so serious i though they were only letting out drug offenders but i was very happy they let me out now it's time to get to business. Ok we getting close you want me to drop you off at your mom's house right. No take me to overtown my crew meeting me there i told you before im taking my shit back a.s.a.p. im not playing no fucking games. Ok cool when you got everything set up let me know and me and my young gunner Ryder will meet up with you and set up how we gonna put this work in your hands so you can get rich. Ok king cool stop right here oh yeah by the way i know you have coke and weed but what about that boy the heroin. Yeah i got that to but i only give it to people who really got shit popping already i can talk more into detail when we meet up check this out i'm not gonna stop right here i will stop 15 blocks from here i have my car parked in the area because i knew you would want to hit the area first. Ok cool my nigga its about to get real and don't worry i know all your area's so i know not to hit your shit. Ok cool here's my car so get up with me when you are ready i'm out. Ok King later. Let me hit the ave and show these niggas Just is back my crew should be there. Ok guys let me introduce myself for those of you that dont know im Just i'm giving you bricks of coke at 12k a piece and heroin for 75k a brick i give you the work you pay me if there is any issue you call my lieutenant Killer B if its nigga fucking with you or tryna war then i'll send the Mob thru and kill everything moving this is the new way anyone don't like it speak up or get the fuck out this is my shit the whole overtown. Mac,Elroy,C-B, and Dat-cre any you niggas gotta problem whats up Dat-cre you got something to say. Yeah who the fuck you think you are bitch nigga coming home after a long stretch like you running shit these bitch niggas is weak they wont say shit but. Hold that thought big man your mom is dead soon as i give the signal your whole crew is dead or down with us now so choose your next words carefully because i got shooters at all you niggas shit and if i don't call in the next few min it won't matter if u down or not bitch nigga matter fact Killer blow that nigga shit back. BOOM,BOOM,BOOM,BOOM, 50 cal desert eagle look at this nigga no head that shits gone anyone else got anything to say if not get the fuck outta here now. Ok now them niggas gone Killer get the clean up crew in here to get this body outta here ok Just but what you think about those niggas you think we gone have issues. No not really but just to cross all t's and dot all i's keep all of them close so if another acts up we wipe out his whole bloodline. Ok Just also i set up the meeting with King at the mall that way everyone can feel safe and get this business done. Ok cool what time is it? It's at 430 and it's 355 now so we gotta be out. Ok call the clean up crew then we out. (ring,ring,ring, hello who's this. Yo dave's Killer clean up at 1457 on 2nd ave you got that. I got it k. Ok come on just let's be out to the meeting. A yo king we have to go, the meeting is set at 430 ok cool lets go Ryder. Aye Just i told King we wood meet at the food court by popeyes ok lets order and wait. Excuse me miss can i get a 2 piece special matter fact make that 2 two piece specials and 2 sweet teas light ice. Yes sir would you like that to go. No, we'll eat it here. Ok your order comes to 15,76. Here you go. Ok your change is 4.24 cent. Ok thanks aye Just let's sit facing the door in case some b.s. Pops off yeah you right but you strapped right. Yeah I got the 44 bulldog on me and I know you got the glock 45. You got that shit right homie or no homie shit go left i will pop any one of them niggas speaking of them there they go. What's up Just this my second in command Ryder what's good son i'm Just this my lieutenant Killer B lets all sit you hungry King. no thanks to my girl cooking later. Let's get down to business so you get your hood back. Hell yeah and it wasnt no problem niggas is weak they not built for leadership material they more like hoe's so i did what pimps do took they money so them some game and put them bitches on the street to work. Dam son i like your style. Thanks Ryder. So King, let me be blunt, my spots can move about 60 bricks of girl a month and 150 bricks of boy. You letting me have the girl at 8k a brick on the strength of showing me love and I'm letting them go. Hold up Just let me interupt my nigga what you letem go for is your business you gettem for 8 because you my nigga so lets keep it G. alright my nigga you got that so you letting me get the boy for 50k thats a total of 7,500,000 for the boy and 480,000 for the girl that 7,980,000 a month total is this shit sounding right to you my nigga. Yeah everything is good Just every month my guy Ryder will make sure the drop off to your guy Killer go smooth on our end then your guy makes sure everything is straight on your end is that G for you Just,Killer hell yeah King sounds good to me what's you think Just Killer you already know whats understood dont have to be said. So known for the payments, King. Payment will go thru this little check cashing place i got on the east when you on your way they will clear out regular foot traffic and then you come in drop off the money and if you get tired of going there i have another one 10 blocks from the pork- n- beans neighborhood and don't worry i have security all round an in these places hidden and all they do is kill when shit go left also call me on this burner if there is any major emergency or you get into something you can't handle, hold up King i don't need you for no beef i'm a certified real goon i'm good,just wasn't't' tryna disrespect but everyone needs some help sometime. No problem, we are good. Ok anymore questions if not me and Ryder have to be out .Nah son we good. Ok killer, nice to meet you. Be easy. Likewise.

CHAPTER 3: JUST INCREDIBLE

Yo Just! King seems to be a real nigga he looked out for real on them birds you must have really held son down in prison. You muh fucking right we was fucking niggas over bad when they cross but that nigga is a different type he really did everything he said he would so on the strength of that alone if he need me or the team for anything we coming thru and mopping shit up. I feel that aye lets go shopping since we about to be some rich nigga. Cool, let's go." Lil spade I didn't want to come to the mall today. Why are we here? Bitch cause i said we were coming that's why. Who you calling a(smack) Now see what you made me do stay in your place bitch now lets hit the guess outlet, yo hold up Kiki i cant believe my fucking eyes isn't that the old head just over there standing by Kiler B. Oh shit babe it is how is this nigga home i thought they gave him life for killing your uncle Ace. that nigga gone wish they gave him life cause I'm bout to take his life (clack, clack,) Hold up babe are you fucking crazy we in the fucking mall with security and cameras everywhere when you off that nigga you want to get away with it. Dam babe you right see that's why i keep yo lil ass around this dirty nigga tortured my bro now don't get me wrong bro violated like hell but he didn't have to torture him then to make matters worse he was goanna off his mom duke and my lil ass and the whole fam i was just a kid and since he was carrying it like that i made a promise to the fam if i ever got a chance i would rock that nigga to sleep now that he home i assume he took back over Overtown because once a hustler always a hustler. I got some contacts over there Ima holla at my man Mac and see what's good so i can get a line on that nigga and get at him but I'm not gone torture him Ima blow his fucking head off. I had to take over Unk shit at 15 years old a kid amongst men but i learned quick the streets got no love i had to be brutal 10x more than anyone to get my respect being a youngin controlling the ports and suburbs while them niggas on the other side control the hoods i had the high class dollar i did shit just as brutal as other niggas but on a quieter level because i was dealing with a whole other element of the game the rich white people. bro was warned not to beat Just out that work because the man was known to do just about anything for revenge but bro thought he was weak and you see he was wrong but i promise i won't make that mistake and get caught slipping. All the nigga Just had to do was killem and everyone would have charged it to the game but no this suicidal ass nigga had to torture him and for that we can't breathe the same air Kiki! lets go i have to tell the fam i saw this nigga he's back now he gotta go. Yo just what the fuck you looking at. See that lil nigga heading out the mall that's Lil Spade i killed his uncle Ace of Spades and he's been watching us for about 15 min so I'm goanna assume he on some bullshit and Tryna contact his people so we gotta get ready for war. Damn, we already in some shit you know i love this shit you know how i get down. I let Killer pay for this shit and go talk to the crew so they can be ready. Hey what about King do we warn him . I don't know yet let me think about that.(ring, ring) David called Destiney hello hey Destiney what's up what you doing babe i just got out the shower why u asking. I'm pulling up stay naked. Dam David you must have missed me today the way you fucking this pussy. Yeah daddy missed you David said as he kept eating Destiney out until she came for the 5th time babe i can't I'm done. No flip yo ass over he was hitting it from the back and in mid stroke Destiney started to throw that ass back yeah nigga you want this pussy you got it she put her hands between her legs and grab his balls she knew he couldn't take that and would cum. Oh shit baby I'm about to come your King is about. Destiney turned around off the dick and let him cum all down her throat and said thanks daddy I'm full then they both drifted off to sleep for the next 5 hours. Oh shit babe how long have we been sleeping about 5 hours David why? I'm late i have to meet Ryder I'm like 30 min late. Yo Ryder what's good I'm close sorry homie i was sleep. It's all good boss i just got to the spot how far out are you? I'm pulling up now. So what's up, how is shit going with Killer and Just? To keep it a hundred they moving work for real but that nigga Just is crazy as hell i been hearing in the streets he dropping bodies and if he doing the most like that i don't want it to affect us. Well lil homie i feel you but he wouldn't even let his shit fuck with our thing and if i thought for a min it would i would cut off all ties or just rock his ass but its not like that. I hear you but I was hearing that he's into it with Lil Spade and he didn't even warn us he was .Well first off that's his beef maybe he felt it wasn't our problem either way i will holla at him when i see him. Ok King other than that everything is good. Ok I'm out and remember keep the crew in line no talking shop on the phone. Let me drive to this nigga hood David said out loud to no one in particularly. Yo Just let me holla as you get in. What's good King you look like something's on your mind. What's up with you and the kid Spade. Nothing's up i killed his bitch ass uncle that's the reason i was doing my bid the lil nigga feels some type of way saying i should of just killed the nigga instead of torturing him first plus i believe the nigga was working with them dirty ass cops Malone and Lomax they was keeping close tabs on Ace and i believe they fucking with his bro lil Spade. Just that's part of the game to get cops on the payroll as long as it's no snitching shit I was concerned about because of the body's. I hear you homie but my thing is my thing. Yo son but how bout this i hear 12 is the reason you was knocked that they put that shit in your car before hand then when you got busted they acted like it was a tip. Hold up are you fucking saying them to cops that jammed you up back before my time did the same to me? Yeah homie that's what I'm hearing. If i find out that's true then i will bury them where the fuck they at anyway. Well I hear they may be retiring this year I'm not sure. Ok keep me informed but other than that how is the work you getting from Ryder? Oh that shit is 95% pure on the girl and the boy is 100%. Good we aim to please I'm about to be out so be easy and don't sleep on the lil nigga Spade i hear he bout that action. Yeah well we went hit his ass in a few days I got the drop on a location on him. Ok be careful Just. I will hang out with you later. Come on Killa answer the damn phone Just think to himself while dialing Killa. (ring,ring,ring,ring) Damn daddy you in this pussy Killa was tearing up some new pussy he met on the block. That's right bitch take this dick. (ring,ring,ring,ring,) incoming call from Just Killer had his phone set to say the names of his contact. Fuck Just calling now dam bitch hold on. Hello what's good my nigga. Damn homie I have been calling back to back what's good I could have had an emergency. Aye homie I'm fucking this bitch from the ave. hey nigga I'm not some bitch my name is (smack) Shut the fuck up bitch I'm on the phone with my nigga, Go head homie what's good. Look we got a line on that lil dirty nigga LiL Spade he over at some bitch house laying low by the port i want to hit his ass tomorrow night i want the whole Haitian mob there we gone flush his ass out. Slow down homie on the phone lets me 15 min by the spot ok cool. Ok bitch give me some more of this fire pussy and call me next week i got shit to do. Fuck that I'm sucking that 10 inch monster so you can see what this mouth do and have something to think about all day. Damn bitch i like how you cuff my balls (agg,agg,agg,) I'm Cuming damn you nasty bitch you licked it off me and everything come here you my bitch do you hear me Cristal! Yeah daddy, I'm here, I'm yours. Ok I'm outta here have to go meet my people. Ok Just you saying we hitting the young nigga tomorrow with the mob. Yeah that's the plan he at this spot by the port my inside contact told me he's watching him like a hawk so where he go we will know but I'm Tryna kill his ass in that where house he at because i believe he also have a stash there also so we gone link up tomorrow around 6 on the block the mob will e there. Ok just it's all good but look we can't ever be on the phone like that talking about murders i know u don't know you have gone a min and i don't mean to offend you. Hey you not offending me you not no regular nigga you my fucking nigga we good and you're right i have to chill out with that shit. Ok big homie see you tomorrow. Yo David what's good this my girl Cherry. Hello Cherry, this is my Woman Destiny. I'm glad you joined us for dinner. I'm glad to finally meet you David and you also Destiny. Girl sit down I'm just happy to see Ryder with someone now we can all be friends and hang out sometime. Girl I'm so happy to hear you say that Destiny i need some friends i just moved out here from the Atl. Oh yeah my people from there too. But before Destiny could say anything more about her parents he looked at her letting her know with his stare to be quiet about her parents because this girl is from the same town she may have heard of them (she understood and switched it up quick) So what part of Atl are you from. Girl, I'm from College park. Destiny was relieved her parents was from Cedartown and anyone from there know the two places didn't fuck with each other so Destiny told her self she would never bring it up again. David asks hey Cherry so how long you've been out here. I was out here for 5 years searching for a place to put a hair spot and I just finished some college courses. Oh ok that's good you got you a winner here Ryder. Hey David I'm going to the restroom Cherry u coming so the men can talk about their business. Sure, let's go. Ok Ryder they are gone. I know what you're gonna say King and yes from the moment she said that i checked her story out but I'm gonna keep her close homie if i see something not right or you hear something i will kill her myself. Ok Ryder until then we treat her with respect. Here comes the girls. Ok you 2 said Cherry can we order. Excuse me, I'm your waiter Joe. May I take the ladies order first. Yes I will have the baked chicken with mac and cheese and a side salad with white wine. Your turn Cherry i will have the same just with red wine ok ma'am and you sir. Well I would like the steak and eggs with grape juice. Dam king that sounds good let me get the same thing. Ok gentlemen and ladies your meals will be out in 20 min or less. So Ryder what you and Cherry got planned for the rest of the night. Shit homie we gone lay up watch so Netflix and chill what about you big homie? Well I think we probably do the same. Hey real quick while the girls are not paying attention i talk to the boy Just he said officers Malone and Lomax may be reasonable for me being set up with the work in the car and the guns and that they were on Ace of Spades payroll at the time on some real shit i been thinking that fuck nigga ace told them fucking cops to set me up because he was scared of a nigga getting more paper than him. Yeah I hear you King but did you two have any beef? No, So why would old boy do that, He was always on some hating shit Ryder i mean the nigga used to see me and look at me funny i use to think it was because we was fucking the same thot bitch he wifed the ho but i was just using her mouth and i remember she told me he found out and was talking crazy about me but i never paid it no mind because the nigga wasn't no one to be worried about. Damn, if that's true we may have to wipe out all the black spades. Yeah I'm with you on that but I'm going to see what Just finds out and if it's true then maybe but first since he beefing with the lil nigga I'm going to see if he get's to him first i may never even have to lift a finger. Yeah son do it that way oh here comes the food. Dinner is served ladies and gentlemen. Joe i have to say this looks good thank you Mr. King. David, this food is good. I see why their slogan is the best food you can find. Yes Cherry it truly is how is yours Destiny. Oh this is the bomb .com. Ryder? Shit King you don't see my plate, it's wiped clean already. Damn that was a very good meal waiter check please. Hey David let me pay this time you always foot the bill . Ok Ryder do yo thang. Here you go Joe. Sir the bill is 275.00 and you gave me 375.00 did you make a mistake. Joe you earned this thank you for your great service and thank the shelf for a great meal. Thank you sir. Dam Ryder you balling. Stop it Destiny! King would have done the same he always treated us. Ok everyone is ready to go me and Destiny has to get up early in the morning Ryder i will holla at you tomorrow. Ok cool King we out too. Hey babe let me get the door for you ok David hey babe let me holla at you for a min look you know that girl could be a plant out here from atl by Crazy Eddie that nigga is slick so if i find out she is I'm killing her my self and Ryder all ready know what's up he's no dummy but so far she checks out. David I knew you were gonna say that I slipped up babe and said too much but moving forward i will be more careful . No need to trip we on that shit that nigga run atl but he don't run Miami i do and if i have to i will call outta town shooters from my hometown Newark NJ and them niggas not gone play with it but like i said Ryder on it he was a little skeptical when she approach him and was pursing him he usually pursue woman but at the same time we don't wanna off her if she really true and feeling my nigga. Ok David but if she is here to find me I wanna off that bitch myself. Ok you got that shortie. "So Cherry what you think of my peoples you seem to hit it off with Destiny like you two were a long lost family. Oh Ryder stop it i just like her that's all too bad! I mean it's too good to be true how nice they are and what did you say they do for a living again. Well David is into buying properties and Destiny owns some flower and beauty shops. Oh I see they are doing these things. Hey woman, I'm doing my thing too. I know Ryder you have those car lots. Yep oh here we go pulling up at home you still want to watch Netflix and chill. Yes babe but I'm going to shower real quick . ok you go ahead i will lock up and turn on the alarms.

(ring,ring,ring,ring, Hello what's good hey cuz its me Cherry i found the bitch. Good job Cuzzo i was wondering was you gonna call thought you fell in love with that nigga and change your mind on the plan. Well cuz he is a solid dude and he's good to me but it's family before anything. Cherry got off the phone and immediately started crying she thought to herself yeah i agreed to do this but i dint know i would fall in love with the nigga and she didn't Know Destiny and King would be good people now she was to hand them over for her uncles death squad in the next 4 or 5 months and she didn't want to do it matter fact she had to figure a way to warn Ryder without him breaking up with her or even worse killing her she decided she was going to put thought into it before her time frame was up. Hey babe you ok in here looks like you were crying you ok. No, I'm ok. Ok well I'm getting in the bed I'm tired. Ok Hun i will be in in a second. Ryder walked away feeling something was off he already told himself he is gonna have his p.i. Investigate her and if she is good then he would show her the world but if she is not then he will rock her ass. Hey baby you ready? Dam Cherry you look good in that thong. Give me that dick nigga she was slurping licking balls licking his ass hole and everything cherry was trying to lock her man down for real that way when she told him what was going on maybe it would save their relationship and possibly her life. Oh shit Cherry I'm about to. (arghh arghh) damn girl you Tryna whip me or what i love your ass for real. Really babe I love you so much. Cherry I'm tired as fuck you drained me lets go to sleep fuck that movie yeah I'm tired to babe all the work i just put in. hey David we are still watching the movie cause if not I'm tired anyway and i have to go check on my shops tomorrow. Ok babe lets take it down I'm tired ass hell to good night baby. Good night King. Killer you got the troops ready to ride out on this fuck nigga in the am. Damn, I just thought we would hit him at night. No i want to catch that nigga slipping and wipe out most his crew i hear dam near all of them stay there with him to keep him secured. Ok cool the troops are ready and we can kill this nigga tomorrow. Lomax and Malone what the fuck you mean you can't kill this nigga or deliver him to me. Listen i can speak for myself and Lomax we can't go near him we set his man up and look what good that did who knew these to would meet in prison and become friends and on top of that business partners so your on your own on this one if it was anything else we could do you know what would happen if King David found out we put the guns and coke in his car the night before and Lomax called his buddy on the narcotics squad we would be dead before we knew it. Ok you two get the fuck outta hear then this mother fucker killed my brother and you wont even help ok it cool remember that shit next time when you behind on child support Lomax and Malone when you owe the Mob bookies don't come here our dealings are done now get the fuck out it smells like pork in here . Ok LiL Spade have it your way, said Lomax. So Malone how we gone get Money now we not fucking with that black son of a bitch. Fuck that nigger Lomax let me

27

think on it i fuck around and hand his ass over to Just or David and let the niggers kill each other off then that way we can come in and take everything that's left.(click, click) got you two now no private eye is fucking with me now let me send these digital photos to King and Ryder i smell a bonus coming to me for this amazing work of Lomax and Malone leaving a meeting talking to LiL Spade. " David laid in bed looking at his beautiful queen Destiny she was 5'7 and 145 pounds little waist with a ass that could rival Nikki Minaj she was a pretty chocolate sister with hazel eyes that she got from her mom "David laid there thinking I'm gonna marry her ass i will propose soon i hope she like the ring i bought her. "He went to Orlando to Williams Jewelers to buy the most expensive ring they had it was a princess cut 5 carat set in platinum and it was worth every penny of the 3 million price tag he spent on it the diamond was so expensive and flawless he took out an insurance policy on it in case she lost it David planned on proposing the day after Christmas which was her birthday he had it all planned out the would open their gifts from each other on Christmas day but then the 26th her birthday he would make her breakfast and put the ring on top of her omelet and when she found it he would get on one knee and propose to her. 'David what are you looking at destiny was yelling at the top of her lungs Tryna get his attention for the past 10 min. "Oh sorry babe I was thinking about how much I love you. Oh babe that's so sweet. I love you too but I have to get up and go check on my businesses what's on your agenda today. "I'm going to go pick Ryder up and take care of some things. Ok babe i will see you later back home . ok baby David replied but still in deep thought.

CHAPTER 4: LIL SPADE

Yo everybody shut the fuck up! LiL Spade was yelling as he stood at the head of the table observing his crew the black Spades listen this nigga Just been out a while now and i talk to some people over there in over town he offed 'Dat-Cre so that nigga outta here and Macelroy, and C-B are too weak to handle the nigga so my plan is we're gonna bring it to his hood day after tomorrow i got an order of ak's, uzi's,and macs coming in tomorrow when he hit them niggas we coming from both entry points and the alley's that way we will corner them niggas in the middle and wipe the whole crew out after that when the heat die down we taking over their hood is there any questions ask LiL Spade as he stood there in awe of his own self Spade was 6'2 200 pounds of pure muscle his dreadlock's came to the middle of his back which he kept them tied up because he didn't like hair in his face his hazel eyes always got him top choice of all the finest woman and he knew his guys was both afraid of him and respected him because he was good to them and he also knew how to put the murder game down." Aye boss a lanky kid names 2 Gunz spoke up don't they get they work from King do you think if we fuck with them, he will war with us and not to sound scared we can't fuck with King he too strong in the city. 'Bam, bam. bam," See what being a bitch ass niggas get you 3 shots to the head from my 45 now as i was saying we hitting they ass day after tomorrow and hopefully King doesn't feel anyway about it and let us get the work they were getting or if not i we can off his ass to. , yeah, spade. Spade, spade, spade, the gang members were chanting, stroking their boss' ego. ``Yo Just you hearing this bullshit Ryder was asking while hiding at the front of the warehouse close by an open window talking to Just on speaker from a wireless headset." Yeah, i hear them pussies but they won't be hitting shit after tonight we got everyone in place are all the exits covered and the roof. Yeah, Just and we put pipe bombs under the cars in case some of these niggas get away. Ok let's hitem. Killer B spoke into the headset. It's a go kill everything moving snipers go to. "Lil Spade was about to make another speech when he notice threw the window glass close to the top of the building a flashing light when he realized what it was he spinned to avoided it but the bullet from the 30r6 caught him in the left eye and he spun and got hit with another one in the right shoulder he immediately dropped to the floor reaching for his button to open the panic room escape route but before he did he looked to see what was happening to his people and all hell broke loose he saw his crew getting gunned down in front of him he hit the button slid under the podium and stumbled thru the tunnel." Just and Killer was letting they hammers bust but they couldn't find Lil Spade they bust in a back-office room and found his bitch Kiki, aye Just this the bitch that was at the mall with him I'm taking her we can torture the hoe until she tells us where this nigga spots be at. "Good idea homie Just holla back over the chaos that was going on let's get the fuck outta here before them people come. Yo listen up Killer screamed to the Haitian Mob we out job well done. "Lil Spade made it out the tunnel and to a stash car and drove himself to a safe house and called his family and told them to bring a doctor and a 100 shooters he wanted Just dead.' aaagh' he was in agony and pain from the gunshot wounds and he was mad at himself he didn't get a chance to get Kiki out the back if he would have tried he would have been gunned down. "Spade, it's me Doc Brown, I'm coming through the door, don't shoot. "Doc" Come on, I'm hurt badly. No, it's not bad, it went through your shoulder and the one to your eye only scraped it. You're ok here let me finish stitching you up and you take these Percocet's twice a day you should be back to the fight in a month. No way in the hell I'm waiting a month to get back at these pussies.'That's the spirit young man well I'm about to leave you can drop my fee off at the office when you have time. 'Ok doc I got you. Hey, spade we all here coming thru i got all the shooters on deck what should we do. Thanks to Sheila, we went straight at them, we hit their block, and we were gonna make that shit hot everyone ready. "We ready Lil Spade'" ok then go make the news my niggas. "Help me please help, I don't know anything! 'Shut up bitch before i cut the 3 fingers off you got left eye Just this bitch is tuff yeah Killa she a top-notch hoe to, but enough games give me the circular saw. (rrrr ,nnnn) the saw was loud and Kiki eyes was bucked as hell when Just put it between her legs. Now tell me what i want to know and i promise i won't kill you bitch. "Ok ok ok you win he has a safe house on downtown flagger St. 1945 that's it that's all i know. "'see bitch I'm a man of my word i won't kill you killer off this bitch (no,no,no,no,) bang, bang, two shots from the eagle and the bitch head is off her body dam Kiler that's a fucking cannon for a gun. Yeah, this shit goes hard aye Just let's go dump her body on the nigga steps on some petty shit good idea then when we done let's swing thru the block i told the young ins to be on the lookout cause that nigga not dead. "LiL Spade and the black spades were in Overtown and had the whole hood surrounded aye you niggas get ready they posted on the block hustling Lil spade was talking to his crew threw speaker phone on his I phone we about to hit i want everybody i don't give a fuck who it is. "But little did he know the Haitian Mob was ready; they had snipers on the roof and had the black spades in sight.(yo Just, Killa them niggas is here spoke they block runner Mack-o thru the blue tooth head set at Just and Killa B yo son we Just burn down all they shit over here and left his girl on the streets in front we won't make it but hit them niggas now.(blattt,blatt,boom,boom,boom,) the fuck they know we here Spades hit back screamed Lil Spade thru the phone let air these niggas the fuck out. (boom, boom,)k dammit screamed Lil spade they shot my fucking phone out my hand bitch ass niggas got snipers i should have waited before i hit them and got more prepared this old head ass nigga is a problem retreat everyone retreat he yelled loud as he could almost damaging his vocal cords and hoped his crew hall heard him he ran back to his black Sabb jumped in and got the fuck outta there hearing sirens in the background." shit let me go to the safe house and wait on the crew pulling up he said what the fuck it's on fire jumping out the car he saw his auntie vanessa." what's good nephew them niggas hit over here and worse than that they dumped Kiki body and one of our look outs said it was just and Killer fuck auntie we gotta regroup at the other safe house this shit isn't over I'm gonna plan it out and I'm gonna finish that old nigga once and for all on everything i love. "Yo Just King on the phone." hand that shit to me what's good King, you tell me playboy word on the street you been teaching the young boy a lesson in who running shit congrats. yeah, that Lil nigga underestimated me i hear he is regrouping some where we will find out where and finish his ass for good. "Do me a favor? What's that King put 2 in the nigga for me i just got confirmation from the p.i. That he was with them cops Lomax and Malone they had some type of argument, but it doesn't matter now he has to go, and I don't care how he dies or who kills him as long as he dies and I'm gonna get them cops and disappear they ass.' Yo king those are cops, so you better be careful they're never found." oh they won't be trust on that be easy Just I'm out.'Ok King I'm out.

CHAPTER 5:
DIRTY, DIRTY

Lomax and Malone were best friends they did everything together from a young age Lomax was 12 Malone 14 they were from Colorado a racist town called boulder they hated blacks and jews at a young age their parents both were in the Klan and they wanted to do everything in life to get rid of the scum they considered black, Jews and other minorities they ended up moving to Miami straight out of high school together and decided once there the best way to rid the earth of anything that wasn't the pure white race was to join the force in Miami Dade police force which at the time they joined it was called the public safety office in 1981 and was later named changed twice until they settled on Miami Dade once in the academy they excelled quickly and threw contacts they landed a job as partners in Miami Dade. It's as though they wasted no time coming from a racist background they fit right in Miami at the time was known to be the cocaine capital of the world they had a record 573 murders in 1980 and in 1982 the first seven months the murder rate was 296 time magazine published their famous paradise lost cover and named Miami a crime infested city with no hope it was the time of the violent Medellin cartel with Pablo Escobar in Columbia pulling the strings and the violent Griselda Blanco in new York and later Miami killing people at will. Their first year on the job Lomax and Malone racked up an impressive 200 arrest out of those 95% were African American or other minorities only 5% percent were white they had a saying if it's black lets send they as back to Africa that is and if it's jew let slaughter they ass and let them stew. An average police officer salary when they started was 40,000 today it about 54,000 they looked at this meager income as another incentive to break the laws they swore to uphold it started small they would arrest small time dealers and give them a choice of going to jail for their drugs or giving up the money and their stash then after they got bored of that they started helping some drug groups move their drugs safely thru the city and sometimes the state and even though they were racist to the core they felt like the ends justifies the means they eventually started working with a local kingpin named Kevin spade aka. Ace of Spades who ran the drug gang the Black Spades who for years went unchallenged he got some of his work from a guy he despised named Just who he would later get a kilo from but was really trying to find out info on him to set him up with the dirty cops on his payroll Lomax and Malone the plan was to lure Just somewhere and have him bring more kilos so they would arrest him but the plan went away when he underestimated Just lust for violence and just killed him so Kevin ended up dying a horrible death by the hands of Just and years after his death his teenage nephew took over the gang after his lieutenant Half-dead got a life bid but some say that he still calls the shots thru the youngsta. Lil Spade pick off from where his uncle left off and decided a local kingpin David King or Aka. King David as they called him was too much of a threat and had to go but that plan ended up backfired because he did only 5 years after his top flight lawyer proved the drugs was planted because David had secret cameras placed in all his cars and although the cops put the drugs and guns in the car they were smart enough to where mask so on the recovered video tape the prosecutor and judge could only see it being planted but not by who. "Lomax i hear there's a war going on Malone was more asking than telling, yeah i hear it's that black bastard Just an that nigger that fired us Lil Spade i hope the black bastards kill each other that way we can com in and pick up the pieces did you come up with a plan yet or any ideas Malone because if not i got one. "Well actually i have we could either dirty them both up put drugs on both of em or we could fake an arrest and kill em both, 'Are you fucking outta your mind Malone we got internal affairs up our ass on some of our past cases the fucking F.B.I. snooping around and not to fucking mention we already got Just ass before like that so twice by the same cops who's suspected of being dirty hell fucking know and that black basterd Lil Spade has dirt on us if anything i hope Just kills his ass or they kill each other.Dammit Lomax your right im a little out of it right now with all this b.s. Around so maybe the best answer is to let the fuckers kill each other then we sweep i an clean shop it would make us look somewhat innocent and it may get the heat off our back. 'yeah that's right Malone it would but we may still need a little insurance we may need to think about talking to King so we can used that as a back up plan. Let's take a drive over to little Haiti i hear there's some new dealers out hustling most likely for king and i need some money and some things for home"" yeah me to Malone i can use some money after that last shake down i couldn't get much the force is watching us closely but today we're out here on our own. Dammit Lomax this fucking car the whole time making clanking and rubbing noises and the department wont switch it out but look at this shit over here in lil Haiti porches and Lambo's parked out in the open they have no shame black sons of bitches there is G-man going in the cigar shop lets get him. (freeze nigger) "what the fuck i do officers, racist bitches! You was born that what you did nigger and lets cut to the chase I'm Malone this is Lomax either you give up the money or we plant shit on you your choice." Hold up partner ! he has another choice we can throw his body in the fucking port of Miami also. 'look man no need for that i have about 8g's on me take it. " See that shit Lomax we took that black bastard money and he didn't put up a fight and he won't know why? Because no one will listen to a know drug dealer even if he goes to the Department which he want he has to prove it now let's split this and be outta here .'Ok Malone since our shift over drop me off at home and pick me up 7am before the crack of dawn tomorrow." You got it partner." Dam the birds are the only thing you here out here the sun isn't even up yet i guess it's true what they say Lomax the early bird gets the worm make the call to King nigger and see what he says ok partner (ring,ring,ring,) hey Destiny don't speak I'm about to get on the phone with the two cops that set me up they got my number out of G-man phone yesterday when they shook him down dumbasses thought he didn't Knows' babe I'm about to go to work anyway. Ok babe later, Hello who the fuck is this, King I'm detective Lomax and my partner here is beside me we have you on speaker phone .Ok i don't talk to cops you want my lawyer number. 'Look dope dealer we not gone play with you meet us out by the port. " no fucking way will i meet any police on their terms i will meet you in coconut grove by the city hall building i will be in a black on black 7 series BMW you pull up beside me and the passenger get out and sit in my passenger seat i don't want both you mu fuckers in my car smelling like pork that shit will be hard to get the smell out i will be there in 15 min you late i leave and whatever you gotta say better be good."(click) .fucking nigger hung up Malone thinks he's really running shit. "For now he is partner for now Let's go so we don't miss him.(knock, knock) what's up Ryder just in time I'm going to meet the crooked police that set me up and see what they Tryna get out ya boy. Shiiit King little do they know they on borrowed time ha!ha!ha! You got that shit right I want you to sit in the back while one of these dirty mu fuckers sit in the front come on out. "Malone there is a car over there pull up beside it. Ok let me get out and talk to him Ok King I'm Lomax, wait i though it would be us who the fuck is this in the back. Don't worry about him you said you had info for me so talk." I have info on how you can get to Lil Spade. We know all his spots but more specifically where he lay his head every night and if you want to kill 2 birds with one stone you can take out the other competition. We even got info on the guy he's at war with Just also, and all we want is 25,000 grand a piece for the info. "First thing copper, Its detective King show me respect, "What fuck your respect you racist piece of shit you think i give a fuck about you two dirty mu fuckers want I'm King i say who get what and when and where if i wanted anyone they would be touched i don't need you to show or tell me shit now get the fuck out my car before you can't," oh,oh,oh,ok, King if yo change your mind here is my card and I'm sorry if i offended you but me and my partner can be beneficial to you we know info on bust on the feds and everything, 'You know what copper i may take you up on that now get out.' Hold up Lomax let them niggers pull off first, ok what he say.' that fuckin nigger is arrogant he was talking about he run this and that and he don't respect us and a bunch of tough guy shit but at the end of our talk i believe he came around. See Lomax what i tell you about them people you have to make them think you on their side believe you me Mr. king will reach out and when he do we will use him up them finish his ass when we're done with him now let's go we got other shit to do like keep track of Lil Spade when he call." Aye King you punked the shit out of that cop. Yeah this mu fucker had the nerve to think we gone work together but little do he know I'm gonna lure they ass out and then we gone slaughter they racist ass."King when you do let me be part of the hit team that guy rubbed me the wrong way and what the fuck he was talking about setting Just up for us. 'Ryder them two idiots are to caught up in they own shit to realize Just is on the team, 'so are we gonna warn Just that they tried to hand him over," I may speak with him on it if i now for sure if he can't get Lil Spade but i will speak to those cops and find out where Lil Spade lay his head and pass that info on to Just. Ok cool my nigga where we going to now, I'm going to drop you off don't you have a meeting with Killer in a few, yeah i do its at 7 and it almost time now they moving weight like a mu fucker bro, cool handle that Ryder and don't say shit about those cops, come on bro what's understood don't gotta be said, cool here's your car I'm about to go scoop up Just and see what's good. " What's up homie? What's cracking Killer you been picking up the pace lately now you fucking moving 150 key of the boy and that white girl. i don't know how you and ya man Just do it in the middle of a war but i respect that's shit to the fullest my nigga. "On some real shit Ryder we been doing the dam thing pushing this shit making these niggas work for us working they ass off now we in war which i personally don't like but the game is the game and it is what it is the young boy Spade all in his feelings over his uncle if he was to sit and think he would realize that his Unk was in the wrong he know dam well out here in the streets u can't let a nigga take nothing from you especially no work and let that shit slide the nigga was outta pocket and he paid with his life. 'I hear you my G but the young boy he got soldiers and he feel like he strong i think he not thinking but you and Just got that nigga under pressure but i hear from my contacts in the Miami Dade police force the feds in town for that exact reason ,so King cut all meetings out until the heat die down i think he about to holla at Just and tell him the same so right know its me and you gonna be doing all business from now on. "Aye mane it's all good we don't want yawl mixed up in our beef but I'm telling you young boy gone fall he in over his head but enough about that bullshit lets get to the money and I'm out i will holla when I'm ready for another reup we good Ryder. 'we good Killer."Yo just what's good son, "shit it's all good King we moving them thangs I'm controlling my shit how you doing. I'm good here. The young boy tried to get at you but failed badly. Also my contacts are saying the fed in town and i got Ryder cross town meeting with Killer telling him what's up on this shit to. "Yeah King the dumb ass lil nigga tried to take a shot at the inventor of this shit and gonna get bodied i know where he at as we speak but I'm Tryna be easy for know we got so much heat on us and i don't want you or anyone else getting caught up in my b.s. But trust in this I'm gonna end his ass real soon. "Let me know even though i asked before if you need me i got shooter outta town in my home town of Newark south orange Ave live nigga will come thru and lay all them niggas down aye matter fact them cops that set muh'fuckers up gone try and holla at me talking bout we can give you Lil Spade and for a bonus Just to i sat and listened to the dumb fucks they don't even know we on the same team all they did was confirm that they been down with they boy and his Unk for years they shit Musta went sour now the kid an't fucking with them now they wanna jump ship i told them racist crackers get the fuck outta here with the bull shit but if u didn't just say u already had a line on the kid i would use them two for the info on where he at and passed that shit to you." Nah my nigga i got this but thanks anyway what's been good with you and your shortie since you touched down. 'We good she doing her business thang and I'm running around tryma get my Lil man Ryder in position to run shit while i fall back and get married and have some lil rugrats running around. 'Oh word the King Tryna have a family dam homie we really out here getting money and getting our family shit right." fa sho homey aye look speaking of my shortie i gotta get outta here and head to the crib she said something earlier about somebody being nosey or or something i will holla at you stay low and be safe." Ok King you to." Destiny I'm home." finally David i been calling and texting for over an hour this shit is serious. 'Slow down babe and tell me everything."Ok i was at my shops and i saw a blue Lexus following me ."wait babe a blue." Let me finish King before you interrupt i saw it so i said to myself girl you tripping so i stopped got gas then went to subway got a sandwich then i did as you taught me i ran the light double back and the Lexus past by the other side of me trying to catch up but didn't know i double back so when i passed them i saw with a quick glance Cherry. 'Babe how can u be sure you was driving fast and' 'this is how the fuck i can be sure David the driver plated on the Lexus had C.E.W. on it them lame Atlanta niggas had Crazy Eddie Crew put on all they shit in abbreviation remember our p.i. Found that out years ago. Damn do you think they followed you here matter fact it don't matter pack yo shit we going to the resort spot no one knows about and let your managers run the stores i wanna see if this is a legit threat before i start killing everything moving why you looking at me like that woman." Well maybe i didn't see cherry and i thought i did and the plates could stand for something else. 'See what i mean Destiny why we have to be sure because once i put in the call the crew will kill everything but fuck that pack yo shit we still gone lay low for that reason and because of this war just is in so to be on the safe side we out this spot and it will go on the market before week's end. "Ok David I'm going to pack now should i pack all your too. 'Yeah do that while i pack the money out the safe up let me make a call real quick to Ryder, (ring,ring,ring,) Hello, 'Ryder its King, 'what's good King. 'look destiny had a scare remember what i said to you earlier about? "Ok i follow you King. 'well she thought seesaw old boy from atl and thought yo peeps was with her she can't be sure so we moving to the other spot only you and us know about to be on the safe side ." Ok i got it." Also she thought old girl was with him in a blue foreign L dog but she's not sure i think it was about 330 a little before our meet. 'Nah King i think she wrong on old girl the reason b is because i dropped her off at the mall before me and you went to the spot and i never called to say meeting over i just showed up at the mall and she was where she supposed to be but you tell Destiny i got it I'm on it watching everything fa' sho ok homie."Cool stay easy i will holla at you later Ryder. "So what he say David." i think he saying old girl been with him most the time even before the meet you know we was talking in codes you never know who's listening but he watching her ass closer he wanted me to let you know he on it but if i know Ryder like i do he will take her life if he see anything that doesn't line up with her. 'Whew! Thanks babe that relaxes me a little let's go I'm all packed. 'Why are you asking so many questions babe? You know you dropped me off at the mall and i shopped the plan was to meet at the food court you didn't give me no time and i was there when you showed up out the blue with no warning you was on your way at all what's good you don't trust me."Ryder looked her dead in the face and lied oh no babe i trust you on everything i love babe. 'inside his heart he cared for her but his mind was sharp and he knew something was off he thought to himself if she don't take my side and tell a nigga the truth she will leave me no choice no matter how much i care for her i will kill her to protect what i have aye Cherry I'm about to go to a meeting i will see you when i get back."Ok babe dam he finally left she thought to her self i have to tell him soon because i know he's getting suspicious and i know

King and Destiny are to my mind is made up i love him to much i just have to figure out how to say it with out him snapping and going off the deep end."Yo bro i got the P.I. on it he's gonna follow her for a bit and let me know what's good King & Ryder but hopefully she is on the up and up or either she loves you enough to let you know what's really good how is everything going on the other thing. "Shit is smooth King i spoke to Killer and he will keep me in the loop i got him calling me on a separate line for any shipments so we don't get tangled in any thing with them but i tell you homie them people in town and they snooping my guy tell me they looking at Lil Spade and maybe even Just but either way I'm playing it real close. 'Well i spoke to just when i had you talking to Ryder he said he about to finish the young boy off but if i even think it or my contacts even say it's a possibility we may be link o they shit i will cut all ties and if it came to it fam or no fam i will get rid of all them nigga cause i really don't agree with how they handling they shit but i don't want to get in another man's problems. "Yeah I hear you king that's what's up so how are you and shorty holding up? She good but i got her on point i don't want any slip ups you know how it goes niggas always get caught up on a humble and I'm not trying to get jammed up for no shit i done and for sho not no shit her peeps did years ago but on the real i think we gone have to reach out and touch old boy since he think he Crazy I'm gone just erase his ass that way i don't have to worry on it no more but look let me get outta here i got this Chinese food I' taking back to the crib i get at you later.Ok big homie.

CHAPTER 6: FEDS ARE IN TOWN

Detective Johansson finally got his wish, kinda sorta the feds approached him about being deputized and he could work as a federal agent they told him they would put in a good word to keep him on permanent if he could take down some of the big drug dealers causing so much havoc in the city namely Just and his Haitian mob and Lil Spade and his crew and if for some reason he could grab King David they would love it even though they knew he was to low key and dam near impossible to nab it would look real good to clean Miami up." He accepted the assignment quickly. He wanted this ever since he joined the force his dream was to eventually join the F.B.I. all he wanted when he was a boy growing up was to be in law enforcement as a kid he saw killings and drug dealings and he knew then he would choose a career in helping to clean up the community when he joined the forced he quickly realized how corrupt it was he saw bad case after case of police like Malone and Lomax trumping up charges on people and he hated that he became a police to uphold the law not break it he even confronted the two dirty cops at one point and him being 6ft and 218 pounds and an avid black belt knew he could kick they racist ass but the crazy thing is even though they hated black people they respected him because he wore the badge like him but to Johannesson it didn't matter badge or no badge if they got in his way he would take them down to. 'it had been months he was following Just and also had a detail on Lil Spade." from what he saw Just was well insulated but from what he heard from snitches in the street he was violent and killed anything not down with him he also believed Just knew he was following him because of the driving maneuvers he saw him do sometimes but Lil Spade on the other hand seemed like he was running the show on the other side of town but in taking a step back he realized that someone else was pulling the strings for the young man and he intended to find out who it was and arrest them also he felt like Lil Spade was a better arrest because he may could flip him and get a lot more people he already knew from following him that he was or is dealing with Malone and Lomax to what extent he didn't know he could be paying them for info or he could be their snitch either way he would be careful as to not give any indication he was on to Lil Spade or the cops because he knew if anyone found out he could be killed without a moment's notice so you vowed not to reveal to anyone he was working with the feds i'm going to take them all down i will put more surveillance on Just and Lil Spade and hopefully i will catch them slipping it's been very hard they are seasoned criminals that know the ends and outs of the law matter fact let me call my team, 'team 1 team 2" check 1' yes we're here ok team operation Just watch is a go we do surveillance and each team try to get hand to hand or any contact with the top guys Just, and Killer and Lil Spade and any top black Spades write everything down any major developments you report back to me and be careful these guys will not hesitate to kill you and one more thing i handpicked you guys because i trust you so breaking the law we're the good guys there the bad guys remember that also the only one that knows about this operation are the feds, me, and the captain so if any of you are on the streets you will be look at like street guys from any other cops with that said are there any questions team1,"no sir' 'team 2."no sir."Ok let's get to it over and out. Johansson sat thinking to himself."Ok I got all my teams in the field, and I got Davis and Vine should be pulling up. 'beep,beep."Oh good there they are.' Davis and Vine reporting sir good let's get to it the teams are out in the field you two will work directly with me on watching over the whole operation and also trying to get a line on King David and let me tell you he's a slippery fish but i have to hand it to Lomax and Malone if it wasn't for their dirty stop an planting shit on the man we wouldn't be on him now the department Tryna clean up its act to save face before they get rid of them to dirty ass detectives. 'Davis, Vine do you have any questions about the operation, well sir i can't speak for Davis but I'm ready to take them all down a.s.a.p. "Sir I'm on the same page as Vine these groups have torn this city apart long enough and it's time to lock them up and lock the city down and get rid of all this unnecessary crime ever since Justin Clark came home the city has seen 200 murders in a year and not to mention Lil Spade is back on the warpath after being calm for years they for sure have to go and as far as King from what i gather he is trying to fall back so unless we truly catch him slipping it will be damn near impossible, 'Vine, Davis your both right and I'm up for the challenge hell!, the whole team is ." So, Johannson is me and Vine to monitor all the cases or are we just on the King case and if we are on all cases who will be the lead when it's time to present it to the d.a. Besides you. Good question Davis but it basically like i have it set up team 1 will do the case and so on now far as the King case I'm head and you guys will get the shine that's what i been saying this whole time make the cases and get them to stick no matter where it leads if there are crooked cops then so be it but we are not dirtying no one case up and if i thought one of my officers which i don't was doing anything wrong i will locked them up to the fullest extent of the law because at the end of the day I'm deputized as a federal agent and so are you so with that said let's crush these guys and clean the streets of this criminal or organization! 'I'm tired of the King's of this world sitting back like he's not doing anything wrong while he pulls the strings but on the outside looking like a businessman but really is the one controlling the city and I'm tired of the Just's of the world killing at will and thinking he's untouchable the dirty cops on this case Malone and Lomax they have to go also it's cops like that they make the community not trust us and i don't care what it takes me you and the whole team are going to wipe not only Miami but Florida as a whole clean of the criminal element that thrives here and i won't rest until i take them all down not to mention my goal was to be a federal agent now even though I'm just deputized at the moment like we all are I've been promised a good word will be put in to the top brass and normally when someone speaks up for you on the inside of the F.B.I. it goes a long way rather than you Tryna to take the test to get in so with that said let's take these mother fuckers down and make our mark in the city and this state ! Are there any more questions Vine, Davis "no sir' no questions". Ok let's begin operation Just watch.

CHAPTER: 7
CRAZY EDDIE

Crazy Eddie is back in motherfucking florida! I love yelling that shit at the top of my lungs that was a fucking 9 hr trip pass me the phone Tash so i can call my cousin Cherry and see what's good."hey Eddie i dont think lil cuzzo want's to give them up, reason being she may have fell in love with ole boy that dick is a motherfucker trust me i know us women get ahold of a nigga slanging that dick we get insane."i don't give a fuck if that bitch loves the nigga or not we have a mission to get that bitch Destiny and fulfill my promise to kill her ass and torture her like i did her mama and daddy, shit she can stay with the nigga far as i care my issue not with him anyway it's with her but i know im gonna have to kill a lot more people to get to her because my intel found out King is a big fish so that spells big fucking problem for us."Eddie you know you could always jus let it be i mean ole girl was just a baby when her parents tried to rob you she didn't even have anything to do with it we could let that shit slide and be out. "I never thought i would see the day when my gangsta bitch Tash would get a heart and turn pussy i wonder what the crew would think of this version of you."First all Eddie dont play me son you know how i get down and far as the crew them nigga more scared of me than you so they gonna fall in line with what i say now i respect yo gangsta and all but you gone respect mine to and i say that outta love.(smack,) Next time you get outta line bitch i won't smack you i'll kill your whore ass im Crazy mu fucking Eddie i run shit now get her on the phone before i forget ho much love i got for you."Ok Eddie you got that. "Bitch i know i do."(ring,ring,ring,)"Hello, what's up baby girl it's Tash i'm standing here with you cousin Eddie he wants all the info on Destiny and King by weeks end."Tash i thought you said you would kill him."I tried you know how it go Cheery."Look stall him a lil more im not giving them up and i know you tired of his shit our agreement is still intact i lay it all out there for Ryder and King and you get Eddie spot when they off his dumb ass and Tash whatever you do don't tell anyone in the crew they will tell him the only way to make them fall in line is to get rid of him first."Ok Cherry talk to you later."What the bitch say Tash."She say everything a go Eddie when she break away from Ryder this week she will slide thru and give you the info."Ok cool you see the crew is pulling up let's go i want to check out some things and go meet up with my Lil man."Dam maybe i shouldn't have been pillow talking with Lil dee about me and Cherry plan i said it was my plan i didnt say Cherry name but if Eddie knows he dam sure not acting like he do."hey bitch Tash fuck you daydreaming about get Lil Spade on the phone."ok Eddie,(ring,ring) what's good its lil Spade ,"Yo it's Tash we here we want to meet up. "Ok im over by the port stash spot no need to say it over the phone you know where tell Eddie i say everything's ready how long will it take you guys to get here."we]ll be there in 15. 'Ok im out." Ok Eddie let's go he said the stash spot by the port." Well well did you see that Lomax,"i sure did Malone now lets see what Mr. King has to think of us now i bet he pay up a handsome ransom for this info and this time Lomax if he don't we will trade his black ass lift off to Crazy Eddie." hopefully Malone it dont go that way Eddie is to unpredictable and his antics might get him killed this time or even locked up These guys have no idea the feds are intown." fuck em all lets get to this meeting with King i texted him on the burner phone he had someone break in our car the other night and place it. Yo King she said that's everything tell em Cherry,"Look king Destiny i know my intentions were fucked up but i was never gonna sell you out i been in talks with my cousin Eddie's top shotta Tash been waiting for a moment like this to set Eddie up he's too unpredictable and we tired of him i been was going to tell you guys but i knew once i did that my life would be in your hands so here i am and you know it all."First off Cherry we're not gonna do anything to you Ryder loves you and i believe you but from this moment on your either with us or against us. "Thanks King i will never do another thing against you guys Destiny are we cool still."Girl we good i was hoping you would ride with us but we wasn't sure if u was with us or even if u was here to spy on me but now we know everything i feel better and lets just put this behind us and move forward. "Thanks Destiny i love you and thank you,Ryder baby do you have anything to say," I love you but never have this happen again other than that we good me and King are gonna move you and Destiny to a safe place while we get ready for war we have the advantage they don't know or maybe they're assuming but for sho they don't know how we coming and we not gone play with em."I got the driver outside for yo girls me and Ryder about to meet up with the crew Destiny you got two mac 11's and a lot of other guns you good at shooting there is a range at the place show Cherry how to shoot just in case and girls no one will know where u at the limo is dropping you off 2 blocks away then you walk only me and Ryder know the safe house no one in the crew knows and i did it that way because incase they get jammed up and tortured and give up the spot so before you go are there any concerns or questions babe i have none i trust in you completely and i know Ryder got you."Yeah king i'm with Destiny i know you guys got us we good soon as i get to the spot i will start learning how to shoot and defend myself. "Ok see you girls later I need to talk to Ryder about something. "Ok King the girls are gone."Yo Ryder im glad she came around she a good girl"Yeah King i'm not gone lie i would have hated to kill her but for the fam i would have done what was needed to protect us so King how you wanna come at thes niggas."we coming at them live and direct we playing for keeps on all fronts i know your shortie said ole girl Tash knows whats up but i think that nigga Eddie is no dummy he may be on to her that's why i sent the girls away we about to show thes Atl niggas how we do niggas when they come outta town and think they can come at the King.(thump,thump,) hold up king the crew is here." welcome gentlemen i see we got liberty city,carol city,opa locka, little haiti and all the surrounding cites here so let me get straight to it here on board with us is Crazy Eddie he think he can come at Me your King and my kingdom well he got another thing coming we're gonna do what's know as a full court press i want you captains and lieutenants to get all the soldiers up to speed and take all action we u see any of these niggas now the bitch u see up here is Tash if you see her out in the field don't trip shorty our inside man i want to make quick work of these outta town nigga's now here's locations on thier different hangouts i want them all hit and be carful the feds are in town i got to cops on the pay roll that let's me know everything now me and Ryder kept a couple spots off the list we gone hit them ourselves reason being we here he sometimes be at those by him self also be on the look out for Lil Spade even though he hasn't came at us and he at war with Just, he been providing that nigga info so if he dies with him so be it but he's not the focus i want this nigga dead and anyone that can take his bitch ass alive and bring him to me will be rewarded heavily are there any questions." i got one King."what is it Sly?" when we kill these niggas what about the other nigga Just he got the city on fire with his b.s."we will cross that bridge when we get to it Sly right now focus my nigga on the task at hand Ryder you wanna say something to the crew."thanks King fellas let's not be mistaken this nigga is no cake walk in the park he's the real deal thats why we coming straight at him we already got some of our people in play on his ass now as we speak meeting is over. "Are you ready to roll out King?" yeah lets go Ryder. "Yo Eddie my man, what's good? It's all good Lil Spade soon as we kill that bitch and King then i can go back to atlanta and relax."Listen Eddie i been knowing you since i was a lil nigga and my uncle use to send you work out there so when you reached out needing info on the nigga King i felt i owed it to you because my uncle fucked with you, but with that being said your reason for the shit is because u killed ole girl folk now u wanna off her im advising you against it let it go."hold up lil nigga you sound like this bitch Tash from the other day King got you niggas shook! "no need to get disrespectful Eddie we family you can do as u wish but u should know King is nonthing to fuck with he got them crazy ass jamaican and haitian niggas not to metion his right hand man Ryder well word has it he has 300 bodies on his resume and even though you Crazy Eddie you can't fuck with them niggas if i thought you could i would slide with you against them," Your concerns are noted Lil nigga now give me the info so i can burn this city the fuck down looking for the nigga,"Here Eddie everything i know on the nigga is here except where he lay his head at and where his right hand man be i do know word on the street the nigga got his hand in everything so you should assume he knows your here,"Oh i know he knows im here because my right hand Tash tried to make a side deal with my cousin and it almost worked until she slept with one of the crew the nigga had the bitch dick whipped so she told him the plan thinking he would ride out with her but the dumb nigga told me not knowing he gone die to for sleeping with anybody in the crew that's rule 10 you sleep with someone in the crew you die." Hold up Eddie, is that who is tied up in the back? Her and the dude she fucked? "It's time for you to leave Lil Spade i will deal with these traitors now."Ok im out here's my burner phone number only you know this line so if it rings i know it's you be safe out here and don't sleep on King."ok later Lil nigga."well well well Tash you thought you was gonna take over my operation have me killed you and that ungrateful cousin of mine and you John F though by you telling me her plans it would put you in her spot,both you unloyal motherfuckers are wrong make no mistake you gonna die today you bitch for your traitorous ways and you bitch nigga for violating rule 10 no sleeping with the crew, Big Mike get the fuck in here, you two know Mike you brung him in but what you didnt know i pulled him aside a while ago and told him with his expertise on spy shit to watch the crew so what a big surprise to me when he said Eddie when are we gonna check the hidden tapes and cameras and when we did we see you too fucking and this bitch on tape, my only regret is i wish i would have looked at it sooner then i could have tricked that bitch as cousin of mine to meet me but it doesn't matter she will die with Destiny very soon."Ok boss i got all the equipment ready who should i start with first."Start with her since she thinks she a gangsta bitch, Tash where are they hiding what else do you know and dont leave out any details and i promise you i will kill you fast you dont tell well Mike here will make your death news paper worthy so what do you have to say."Ha,ha,ha,ha" Crazy Eddie your lame nigga im straight gangsta (grrrr,spew)."Bitch you spit in my face after all i've done for you Mike start now."Ok boss". (aghh,aghh,help,aaaa,) "dam Mike the blow torch melted the bitch feet bitch you wanna spit now tell me where they at."Eddie on my mother's soul i don"t know i knew talk to (bam,bam,) Bitch you running outta feet and this 45 not gonna run outta bullets i got plenty Mike go."Eddie you shot her feet off she's done really is no use for more but if you insist hand me the pliers."aghh,aghh,no please im sorry help me, Dam Tash i give it to you your tough bitch thats why i put you on the team but my patience is running thin after you die i will find your little sister in the atl and well you know how i get down."Eddie please i never talk to King directly it was your cousin and even if i called her right now she wouldn't answer she threw the phone away she knows you may have me because i never (bam,bam,bam,bam) got back."Now look bitch your little boyfriend is dead and at this very moment i got goons in his wife house running trains on her before they kill her and you say you don't know anything Mike go." This should do the trick (mmp,mmp) "dam Mike the bitch eyeball is hanging out im gonna keep that screw driver for a souvenir so i can remember this bitch had one eye and sit back and laugh at her for fucking with Crazy mu fucking Eddie your times running out i got people that's at the college now waiting on your sister to come out.

(ha,ha,ha,ha.)"bitch what's funny."well Eddie you bitch ass nigga my sister been dropped outta college and i had her move years in advance in case something like this happen your time is up i froze your money in any accounts you had and the mone you had buried i got to it and gave to my sister for a new start knowing that what i was doing was a suicide mission the only way i been sitting here acting like im so scared is i was stalling for time.

(ha,ah,ha,ha,)"Stalling for time for what bitch for what, Mike go."whamp,whamp,"boss this bitch is finish"Yeah laugh now bitch that axe took off both legs to the knee caps."ha,ha,ha" stalling for time Eddie you won't leave here alive the whole thing was a setup you shoulda look at your camera footage sooner.

(bam,bam,thud)"fuck you ho now look at you dead Mike i want you to clean this up and burn these bodies up in that funeral home across town we posted at then i want everyone to be on the look out i dont know what this bitch been saying but we have to watch out for any sneak attacks and we putting etra security at all spots in case king knows them you understand." I got ya Eddie but if you don't mind me saying maybe we should leave and regroup i mean here we are in someone else backyard and they have the advantage Eddie me and the team will die with you but we shouldn't just run to the end we should try to figure things out."shut the fuck up and do what you told mike before you become a statistic."ok boss im sorry im about to get rid of all this your car is in the back i got 4 guards on it so you should be safe when im done i will meet up with you."ok Big Mike then when you come we gone go hit King and see how Gangsta he think he is.("ring,ring,ring) whats up baby girl David we made it safely talk to you soon."Ok babe i love you and Destiny dont worry we got this."Cherry have you heard back from ole girl."No Destiny i think she's dead the plan was i was to destroy my phone because we knew Eddie would have Big Mike bug them and i got the burner on but she didnt call so i fear she is dead but we both knew what the out come would be if caught but what that dumb ass Eddie didn't know was mike records everything so if his dumb ass made it thru this alive Tash sister will have recordings of all his shit starting from when he told mike to record the crew it was all in our plans to get rid of him after while he will be in a war by himself, the crew is tired of him and we been begging him for years to leave this thing alone w he likes to kill his enemy's and there family's all the other hustlers and even connects in the city were getting tired of his craziness so he burned all bridges and he somehow got the cops on his payroll to get the evidence thrown out the killers in the atl have orders to all go at him and this is from the top cartel bosses he brings to much heat everyone knows who King is and no one wanted any parts of fucking over a good nigga so if King don't killem Crazy Eddie is still a dead man walking."dam girl you rally been putting in work to get this nigga out the way and he your people so he must really be fucked up i remember hearing the stories about how he did my parents and don't get me wrong i know the game they had to die trying to rob a top nigga in the city, was a risk and with high risk comes high rewards or even high stakes and i made piece with that but to put word out that you would kill me they little girl at the time and offer a million dollar reward for my where abouts was crazy, so in my book fuck that nigga and the bitch who made him, now he gonna get what the fuck he got coming for fucking with boss niggas, and i thank you Cherry i know how hard it was to give him up and any of his people you thought would come back fo revenge but it had to be done and now you part of the family."Thank's Destiny i needed to here that, but truth be told everyone back home is tired of him he kills at the drop of a dime for no good reason i mean the game is the game and we all choose the lifestyle but to kill niggas over petty b.s. Like this one time a nigga was just smoking and he said you smoking peach black-n-milds instead of strawberry and he shot the nigga on the spot, alot of the shit he be doing is because he started to believe his own hype of being crazy Eddie so he feel he have to keep the crazy shit up and that shit was coming down on his family the nigga dont even care i came to him time after time to treat people fair he pay his workers basically minimum wages but expect everyone to be loyal while he's sitting on millions everyone is struggling to survive so when Tash cme to me with the idea i jump at it Eddie deserves what he has coming to him and he's too caught up in himself to see he will not win but make no mistake about it he will do whatever he needs to do to survive he has turned into that persona Crazy Eddie so when King hits him he better make sure he's dead cause if not he will come back 10 times worser than before."Trust me Cherry King and his guys not gone play with em and when he really catches him its a wrap, it's too bad tash won't be able to see the results i figured just like you did he got to her she's dead." Destiny we both knew what the risk was we made promises to each other so my end was if she died i was to always look after her little sister by sending packages to her once in a while to a p.o. Box and her promise to me was to protect any of my and Eddie's family that wasn't part of him and what he had going on and since she's dead i have to keep my word.(ring,ring) "who is this calling from a block number, "hello" Bitch did you think you could hide from Crazy m.f. Eddie.(click)"Oh shit it was him how did he get this burner number."Wait girl don't panic take out the sim card and flush it and break the phone if he killed Tash the number probably was on her somewhere,"Girl you right let me get rid of this phone."Eddie did she answer yeah the bitch answered Slug and she knows im gonna get her i will cut that bitch into a thousand pieces and cook her and eat her as a fucking pot roast," you and Big Mike get ready cause soon we gone hit King ass im tired of playing with these miami haitian niggas they think because of the dam Zoe pound niggas is scared and not all them niggas be down with that shit they just say that to scare niggas off well i want all the smoke im with the dumb shit, i see Mike pulling up now let's get ready," Slug just looked at Crazy Eddie thinking what the hell i signed up for fucking with this nigga, What's good Mike?" It's all good Eddie i got a line on King he over across town i hear with the nigga Just i wasn't sure did u want to hit him or wait until he not with Just since he not part of our beef." I'm gonna hit his ass and if just there take him out to then all i have to do is get rid of Lil Spade bitch ass to so get ready im going into my office to make a few calls back home to see if all my work i put on the street is almost gone so we can send the niggas another shipment so i will be back out here in 30 min." Hey Mike." what's up Slug, " My loyalty is to you and you only but i think this nigga got us here to die with him you should think about giving him up i hear King got a quarter million on his head."Hold up homie i don't play the game like that if we picked the losing side then we ride this motherfucker til the wheel's fall off i dont break bend or fold im a street nigga and i thought you was too but if there's bitch in you step off but dont let me hear you being so weak again understand."understood Big homie i was just venting im down for whatever i got you." That's fuck up to hear you say that Slug." Oh shit! Eddie how long was you behind me i wasn't going to turn on you i,(swipe,ugg,ugg,) Off with yo head nigga bet you didn't think i could kill one of my homies did you Eddie?"I must admit i don't know if it ever came to it would you but for you proving yourself i'm giving you a five hundred thousand dollar bonus and you gone run my Atlanta operation while im out here running these niggas but first Let's kill all competition see it was about the lil bitch but now it's about taking over everything i bet after this the cartel will give me a seat at the table with this shit over here combined with my operation in the ATL i can easily move a ton of coke and heroin a month." Boss i hear you but it's time the crew is pulling up let's go erase these niggas from the planet and then after that we celebrate on their dead fucking bodies." Ok Mike lets go," Fellas welcome no need to unpack get all your guns ready we about to go ride on these bitch niggas and we wont give them time to regroup or (bam,bam,bam,blatttt,blattt,) oh shit what the hell everybody get down Mike cover me Mike oh shit they shot Mike in the head come on let's get in the warehouse i dont know where they shooting from.

CHAPTER 8: GET THE COPS

Yo king what you wanna handle first i got all the lil niggas in the city on the hunt for Eddie so soon as they got em we will get a call." Good looking Ryder you step up to the plate and turned out to be a good leader we on our way to meet up with them cops i think they know I'm aware of them with setting me up so they been kissing my ass giving me all type of info but truth be told my contacts say the feds in town so i didn't want to kill them just yet it's a lotta heat out here because of Just war with Lil Spade and soon as we get it popping with Crazy Eddie it's gonna be scorching out here," Yeah my nigga your right King but it's the game sometimes you have to go to war but look check this out there go Malone and Lomax. 'Come on Ryder let's step out the car to talk to them. 'Hey Lomax, there goes King right there they are getting out to talk to us they never did that before so keep a close eye if they try to pull, they weapons it will be two more dead niggas on the news. 'Malone how we gone play this straight up like we talk about before." Yeah, Lomax we're gone to see where they're head at with it let's get out and talk to em."Gentlemen you know my right-hand Ryder, so we all know each other we're not strangers so let's talk why did you want to meet today. 'King it's like this Me and Lomax know you heard about us planting evidence on people and we did set you up on the orders of Lil Spade but since then we have realized that his side was the wrong side now I'm coming at you straight up so there is no secrets i know you may feel the need to do something but son i suggest. 'Hold up you piece of shit I'm not your son address me as King and if i

wanted you to be dead you would be and i wouldn't lose a wink of sleep matter fact i would kill you myself so i would enjoy it but asshole i recognize we have a mutual relationship where is i get info and you get paid but make no mistake about it try me you die when you pick the street side you no longer choose to be cops your street guys and if and when i want to i will handle you as such now get to the reason you wanted to meet me out here before i change my mind and take your bitch asses out. Ok King we understand each other first thing the feds are on a wiretap on all of your guys phones they just got approved today now i don't know if you have one because when i looked at the report i remember them saying they couldn't find if you have one or not but i can tell you who heads the investigation it's a detective name Johansson and i can tell you this they promoted him to be a temporary fed for this case and if he does good it will be permanent so you know he's going all out he wants Just, Lil Spade, You and now this m.f. Crazy Eddie's in town the feds took the gloves off they watching everyone even us so you need to protect yourself warn your people because they coming and with a 95% conviction rate they won't lose in court.' well Malone i guess we better not end of in court but don't you worry i got my end under control you make sure you never get followed so next time we meet it will be at the abandoned warehouse across from the port that way you know ahead of time and from now on every meet i will tell you the next meet ahead of time. Ok cool King you can drop off our usual payment in the same spot if it's no problem to you." Your money is already at the spot, let's go Ryder. 'King those two idiots don't know how close they are to dying the doing the typical good cop bad cop act like they in control of something when all you have to do is say the word." Fuck them Ryder i did everything in my power not to blow they shit back but in due time it may even be sooner than later but for now they are telling me necessary info on the feds and all this beefing shit going on in the city one thing fa sho Just gonna have to either kill the young boy or get the fuck out the way shit is getting hectic out here and I'm not gonna let anyone fuck my shit up if this shit don't end soon i will send you to clean up all of it ya dig." I hear ya boss and m ready we are losing millions with this beef shit don't get me wrong Just making his numbers but the other bosses in the city are afraid to make any moves because they fear the feds will hit em." Have you checked on the girls lately?
'No1

king let me call em."(ring,ring,ring) hello!" What's up Cherry, how are you doing? We good Ryder is everything ok on your end?" yeah shit straight babe can you put Destiny on the phone so King can holla at her. 'hello" What's up babe you, ok? "Yes, David we good just wishing this will be over soon," It will be babe very soon but look i gotta go have a call on the other end,'Click'Hello'what's up King it's Sly we got the Crazy guy pinned down at the warehouse what should we do? Stay there, listen to the police scanners me and Ryder on the way. 'Click" Dam King they got the m.f. Pinned down let's get over there asap. 'Ryder when we get over here we gotta not let this mu fucker escape i want this shit to end today. Aye King bet his ass wish he would have stayed his black ass in the ATl now nigga thinking he the only one that can put that work in well we about to show up and show out on his ass.'We almost there get the Guns out the stash box and Ryder get the extra clips we 20 min away." Malone how you think the meet went with King you think he gonna let bygones be bygones. 'I told you before Lomax if he don't we'll plant some more drugs and guns on em the only difference is we'll kill his black ass but hopefully he come around it did seem like he let it go but i don't think we have to worry about King right now he got that Crazy Eddie m.f. Running around then Just ass out here killing everything moving so his plate is full. "All available units we have a code 30 near the warehouse district "copy that this officer Malone and Lomax we're 15 min away no need for a code 15 i repeat no need for assistance," fuck is that Malone it's gonna be where Crazy Eddie at so let me call King and warn him hand me the burner phone."(ring, ring,) What the fuck now's not the time, 'Look king listen we got the call about the shooting at the warehouse district you got 45 min to an hour that's the longest we can hold off the other cops' i hear you! "Click"." fuck he say Malone, Ungrateful black bastard talking about now's not the time stupid nigger I'm giving him the heads up if it wasn't for us the feds would be all over his black ass, Malone please don't trip let's just milk these niggers for all they got then we on our way into retirement." Yeah your right Lomax fuck em." King what the cops say, "they said we have about an hour before it's swamped with they people over here come on let's talk to Sly and see what's up. 'Sly what's good" King we was driving when we got the call from one of our lookouts someone was here at this spot looking like they was having a meeting getting ready for a war so we crept up got the Ar-30's out and started dropping they ass it was about ten men it's only four left now we hit Crazy Eddie in the leg and shoulder but i think he had a vest on the way he was acting was some shit straight outta Scarface like he high as hell or something so depending on what you say we was gonna storm the warehouse and finish his ass off." No, we don't have time. The dirty cops on the payroll says we have an hour and that was thirty min ago do you still think he's in there or did he slip out." I Dunno King but shit i will just call hid name he's crazy enough to reply' 'Aye Eddie you might as well kill yo self your a dead man walking. 'Mother fucker I'm Crazy mu fucking Eddie i done pissed on niggas tougher than you fuck you your mother and that bitch nigga King I'm gonna kill everyone in your families starting with the women this beef shit is nothing to me i love it you made your move now watch mine Sly. 'Oh shit the nigga know my name king" Yeah he's tuned in to the town from Lil Spade running his mouth I'm gonna have to get rid of his ass for being part of this shit anyway that's if Just don't kill em first." Aye King' what's good Ryder? A fucking helicopter landing on the roof and it's not police." Shit he's escaping hand me a rifle Ryder, 'here King" (ping, ping, ping,) what the fuck is the chopper bullet proof."(King, King, King)" this mother fuckers on a bull horn. 'King it seem you underestimated Crazy Eddie now you will pay when i find your bitch I'm gonna keep her as my ho and put her on the street ha,ha,ha,(blattt,blattt,)"Duck King this mu fucker shooting." See you soon King." Yo King dude really Crazy talking about what he gonna do to Destiny." I'm not worried about that no one can get to the girls they not even in Miami but now we can't go near them until this is over and i already text Destiny and told her we can't come near them and to stay low we gotta get this nigga,

Sly soon as you get any calls from the guys watching the other spots let me know we have to full court press this nigga but i want everyone around him dead and i want to cut his fucking head off myself put the word out anyone catch his black ass alive the reward is 2 million now and if they get him call me or Ryder ! Sly you did good keep on the hunt me and Ryder are about to bounce you do the same the cops maybe on their way. 'Dam King Eddie is Crazy as fuck."Let me tell you something an old head told me Ryder everyone crazy until they meet a real Crazy m.f. Eddie's on borrowed time he's done he won't leave Miami unless it's in a body bag because it fa sho won't be standing up. 'Everyone check in this is Sly make sure all eyes are open the Crazy guy got away but the ante has been up to 2 million alive he's gonna head to one of the spots he's in a black-on-black helicopter copy that. We copy, copy, copy,' Ok cool now soon as he lands call me and i call the boss. 'King so what you wanna do now wait for the call or holla at Just," Call Just on the phone he needs to get Lil Spade and we get Eddie kill 2 birds and the city is mine or should i say ours. (ring,ring,ring,ring,) what's good Ryder, Aye Just,' King wants to speak to you, hear you go King. 'What's good Just we just had it out with Crazy m.f Eddie He got away in a chopper dude think he live but we gone see if he can live another week since he bout that life what's up on your end with the Lil nigga." Shit we on something right now as we speak this little piece of shit think he smooth but he fuck up and we on em"Just we need him to go away he was the one who told Eddie whatever info he knew on us but the dumb fuck don't realize a nigga Like Eddie will turn on him the nigga will Kill the Lil nigga and take over his shit but the Kid to green he's not built for leadership material he more like a soldier that's the problem with some nigga's they wanna be the boss but don't have leadership quality. 'King don't worry we got this Killer got a line on em we close to taking em down and stop trippen I'm solid i would never involve you in my b.s. You got enough on your hands with Eddie and we got the word from Ryder so we know the feds in town so go take Eddie down and we gone Take Lil Spade down."Ok Just I'm gonna trust in you do ya thing, I'm about to be out I'll holla at you later." Ok King one" Yo Ryder Just' 'claims he got the Lil nigga in the scope so leave it to him but if he don't get em and the heat come down on us we gone wipe em all out. 'King what ever you say but you know how i feel it's risky waiting on them to handle the shit but i trust your judgment and you the King and it's your Kingdome, "Ryder it's all good my nigga" Did you get any word from sly on Eddie yet we have to find him asap before he do some off the wall shit. No not yet but the boy should be hitting me up soon the whole crew want the ransom we put on his head they even agreed that it doesn't matter who get his ass first they gonna split it between the crew." See Ryder that's what a King likes to see his people sticking together. 'Aye King look over there by the alley over there at the seafood place you see that. 'Oh, shit they are placing what looks like a tracker on them two detective's cars dial them m.f. up. (ring, ring,) Yeah Lomax speaking what's up King where u at ? We over at the seafood spot." I'm across the street and i just saw two feds put a tracker on your car i just wanted to give you the heads ups so you don't get caught slipping. 'Good looking out they keep trying it but we keep catching they ass they wanna catch us bad but we on them, they have our regular phones tapped but don't know about the burner we be on with you. "Ok Lomax keep it like that but be more careful also because we see they not playing that damn Detective Johansson is about his work for them feds' King holla at you later. 'Lomax i blew that bathroom up, 'what did King want some more info. 'No he was passing thru and saw the feds putting a tracker under our car matter fact let me lower my voice they probably got the place bugged and the waiters and waitresses may be feds. 'Lomax fuck em they can do what ever but we cops to so we know all their tricks we check our car and we scan for bugs but you know what from now on we don't even say King name on the burner or out loud just in case they gotta machine that can here threw walls or a lip reader. 'Yeah that's a good idea Malone these motherfuckers and that black son-of -a-bitch Johansson think they so slick if he keep it up we may have to do his ass in to along with King and the rest of em." fuck Vine ,Davis did you get any of that. 'Boss Vine here i didn't get it when i went to the table they stop talking and i did want to stare or stand there to long but they for sure was on the phone telling someone something about feds that's all i got. 'Davis copy, did you get anything. 'Davis here copy the only thing i could here from the bug under the sugar was something about doing something about you or King or both of you and I'm not even sure i heard that right." I wish those two would come for me it would make my job easier but one thing for sure they real slick they know how to cover their tracks real good but all we need is one slip up i don't care if they see us or they keep finding the trackers my goal is to make them so paranoid they break and when they do we gonna be there to scoop they ass up and unless they got some info on murders or some big wig, bigger than King they ass will be doing life and it won't be in Jackson corrections it will be in the toughest fed place the law allows since they wanna be gangsta's then let em be where gangsta's at and i guarantee they won't make it long we been playing with they ass for too long the local police know they dirty but still can't get them in fear of what will happen if they really have ties to the underworld. 'Boss, me and Vine are gonna do everything we can to help you take them down. They outside and found the tracker they threw it away ."Let em pull off then Davis go get it I'm about to pull up you and vine come on. 'Wow look at this sloppy shit right here King the feds pulling up just after Malone threw the tracker away. 'Take a mental note Ryder remember those cars even though i know they have more surveillance might even have some people watching us now while we watching them but no worries I'm parking this 7 series BMW and we gone pick up the Porsche truck Ok Ryder they left let's go get this truck.

CHAPTER 9: JUST & LIL SPADE

Yo Just i got the haitian mob ready they gonna meet us over by lil Spade safe house we gonna surround the Lil nigga to make sure he don't get away this time we almost had his ass last time but fuck all that lets end his ass."Ok Killer me and you gonna be at the front door we will put the troops on the sides and the back and im thinking on throwing some smoke bombs threw the windows to make sure they have to come out lets get the guns ready.(screech, screech) what the Hell!" Just get down blattt", (blattt, blattt,blattt,blattt) pull of Killer im hit motherfucker hit me in the shoulder go to our doc now."blatttt,blattt,blattt," Hold on Just i gotta shoot our way out of this.'('boom,boom,boom,boom") come on that's all you got!" Lil SPade your dead your family's dead your fucking kids dead."Ha,ha,ha," look at these old mu'fuckers run! i told you not to sleep on me you an't no fucking Killer and Just you gone be Just dead,"yo everyone get them old mu'fuckers(blatt,blatt,blatt,) (boom,boom,boom,boom) Just here's our chance i hear them people coming lets go.(screech,screech) Dam Killa don't blow the tires out get us the fuck up outta here the young boy got one past us today but he fucked up make the call hit his people now. (ring,ring,ring,ring,) Yo it's Killa hit the peeps now Just got hit he's ok though."Ok Killa say no more." Ok Just it's a go and we here at doc's the garage is open i texted him while i was driving."Killa" what's up Doc it's not that bad it was in and out."Ok lay him on the table let me begin get the galls Killa."aghhh" Shit that hurts."Come on Just you been shot before and this is not bad."Fuck that mean shit still hurt's like hell."Ok it went in and out you only hit in the shoulder where the rest of this blood came from i dont know,"Killa come her for a sec let me look you over."ok doc but im good i didnt get hit."See right here a Lil pin hole, matter fact2 pin holes look like it was a 22 or a 32 with a silencer on it and your adrenaline was pumping so you didn't even feel it."Well an't that a bitch nigga's hit me Just you hear this shit."it's all good killa that lil nigga about to feel the wrath of cain."Ok gentlemen here are some percocets killa your shit is only flesh wounds take two a day until the bottle is gone Just take three a day."Nah doc we good we don't take any drugs unless we made to your normal twenty thousand will be in your box by tomorrow come on Killa let's be out so we can find this nigga.(knock,knock) yes who is it."It's Cain and Abel my brother keeper's plumbing."hello Sir but i didn't order any work to be done. Are you Lil Spade baby mother and is his kids here."Yes but i dont fuck with that nigga so why would he."swish,swish," Dam Cain the new silencers are quite go to the boy room im going to the girl room.(swish,swish,) (swish,swish). Ok Abel is the upstairs clear because the downstairs is." Yeah no one's here i found thirty thousand in an open safe upstairs i guess she wasn't to mad she took the nigga money."Yeah let's pour the gas all over the house and turn them gas stoves on when i finish Abel go we got other targets then we have to get out the city you never want to disappoint Just."Cain start the car the fuck is you doing!"hold up son (boom) See that's what i was waiting for it does how many jobs we do correct all we need is one job to go wrong then that's our ass all evidence is gone lets go to the next job the warehouse where the so called gangsta niggas at."Yo Spade you was right we hit them old niggas they was running like roaches hit Killa as two or three times and we tore Just old ass up why you looking with the screw face."I been calling my baby momma she not answering she dont really fuck with me unless i drop off some money she said i chose the streets over her but women never understand this shit in my blood."So what you wanna do Spade."Go over there i gotta get her low for a min you know that old nigga crazy they called him back in the day just about anything because he will do anything for revenge."Yo that nigga wouldn't dare touch women and kids what's the address ot's in Coral Gables." Yo Abel there is the spot right there pull over pop the trunk.(click) This c-4 put it around the building i'm going up top to the roof be alert."aye Cain these niggas act like we not at war no one's looking out they underestimate's Just savagery."Look just watch your ass meet back here in ten min." man what the fuck was Spade thinking letting them niggas get away its twenty of us here we coulda been there he talking about wait for the fucking call i'm really starting to question his fucking leadership."Look at these dumb niggas aye Abel copy can you hear me hope this nigga got the raio on."I do i hear you what's good bro."This shit gonna be light work they sitting in here with granades lets me back at the side."Ok Cain thier is no one at the back door." I think the lil nigga told them to stand down did you wear glove when you put the c-4 down. "Come on bro you know i did."Ok let's walk down the block to the car we can watch this shit blow from here.(911) yes caller whom am i speaking to." i rather not say my name sir."Ok caller what is your emergency i'm riding past the warehouse district and i saw two suspicious men walking around and planting things on the ground then one walk to the roof."well sir they could be workers i know they not because what workers dress in all black."Ok sir we're sending officers out there are you in a safe location."Well i'm watching them."Hold up they just pull off and are approaching my vehicle."Sir you need to leave now."Cain you right he on the phone looking at us pull a lil closer open up the sunroof."Hello nosey ass goodby dead ass."(piff,piff) "Hit the detonator Cain. "boom!boom!" "Good thing we blocked the doors look at them nigga tryna get out. "Fuckem Abel get Just on the phone.(ring,ring,ring,ring) yeah wassup twin we over hear in the district and we all the pigeons in the coup except the main one and maybe one or two others all the pigeons are done flying."That's great to hear put your brother on the phone."Yes Just you guys are the best no need to finish the rest only look for the main one and if you find him before me hold him." Ok we got you.(click)."what he say bra!"he want us to get Lil Spade."Killa what i tell you about them twins they official niggas been killing shit since 13 years old i only call them on hard jobs. They told me in code of course they killed all of Spades men he's done and I doubt Eddie will help he's running from King. It's only a matter of time."Hold on the twins texting me. See that's what i'm talking about they kill so much they forgot to mention they got his baby mother and kids."Aye Just thats gonna push him over the deep end he will be everywhere looking for us."That's what i'm counting on once that rabbit stick his head out the ground then ima blow his fucking head off let's vest up and get out here in the streets it's only a matter of time now." Right here Joe."Ok Spade lets clip up and make sure our bullet proof vests are secure."Joe let's go! (knock,knock) What the fuck the doors are open im going upstairs to the bedrooms you check down stairs."Aye Spade yo Spade you need to see this."aghhh" This motherfucker is dead im going for him now."Hold up Spade im coming up stairs."Yo Spade i can't believe this shit what type of low bottom ass nigga does this he violated the code no women and children. And why did he have to burn them."Spade i think he tried to burn the house down but something went wrong the fire went out"He did this to make me snap he thinks i'm a hot head but im smarter than i look."We going off the grid me and you and when we pop back up we killen everything in site you wit me my nigga."Im wit you all the way to the grave if i have to but look i know this your kids and there mother."I know we gotta go Joe they will think i did it since we fought so much let get up outta here."Detective Johansson."Yes Davis!"you know this is the work of Just and his crew i mean he's know to be over the top i can't believe in the middle of war he caught Lil Spade slippen like this it's like over 20 something bodies dead here and there is no fingerprints or really any evidence and the killer or killers used c-4 who does that no one but a professional hit team. Not to mention the witness outside is dead two shots to the head brains and blood all over the fucking car and all alarms and cameras are disabled."Yeah Davis this here is some real crazy shit right here and he got me looking bad the feds saying i dont have anything on him but suspicions. Johansson! Johansson!"Dammit Vine!"fuck you yelling my name for im in the middle of a fucking bloodbath of a crime scene."Sorry boss but across town there is another crime scene and i believe the same killers did that because they used silencers and they killed the damn kids who the fuck does that Just has to go sir he's off his rockers.(ring,ring)"yes Johansson speaking. "I hear you sir,but sir how did,sir hello,hello,"The fucker hung up."What's up boss?"I was told by the top brass if i don't put a concrete case on Just go work for ups because that will be the only job i will be able to get after they bag my ass and make me take all the weight for this fuck up. But they don't understand if it's not there it's not there now i see why Malone and Lomax go the route they take. I mean i'm not condoning it but i understand matter fact they may unintentionally help us."How boss tell me an Vine." It's simple i'm gonna let them do what they do if i catch them on my wire tap or in the act i won't arrest them i will tie them ass up in my case and tell them i have them then they would have to testify on all they saw and did."i hear you boss but wouldn't that be stuping to the criminal's level."Shut the fuck up Vine and let me finish im gonna arrest they ass after i pin them on the fuckimg wall they will have to take a plea agreement or i will lock they ass up in the same prison Just black ass is going to."Now let's go to this other crime scene." This mother fucker killed her Joe he kill my twins he has to go fuck laying low im going on the prowl and killing his ass."Lil Spade we have to think and plan things out never go on anger it wont turn out right. (boom,boom,boom) Die nigga! Telling me what the fuck to do now you dead stupid bitch! Now I'm gonna get you Just im coming for you your a dead man."Yo Just niggas in the street are mad but at the same time they scared as shit they saying we violated the code that was agreed upon never touch family's you realize they may turn on us or come after us right."Killa you wit me right?"What type of question is that im down but we gotta be careful niggas think,"Fuck what they think i will kill anyone that opposes me and that includes King if he feels a way bout this shit i run this mother fucker and truth be told i should have it all but long as they all stay in they place then we good."now killa let's go find this lil dirty ass nigga."Davis,Vine get your ass over here and secure this crime scene i want to make sure it's not contaminated i wnt the fuckers that did this to pay with they life on death row. "Johansson! "Yes Vine i didn't know before but the killers not only burned the bodies they tried to burn the house down but i think they didn't realize she had a fire system in here that kept the flames down enough for when the fire truck an ambo came the fire chief said it was regular gasoline they poured it all over the turn the gas stove on the killers may have heard the water heater blow down stairs and thought the house was exploding but that was just dumb luck it blew when it did then her alarms went off and her fire sprinkler system sprays not only water but some kind of solution that stomps fire i believe foam it had to cost over three hundred thousand dollars to put in."Drug money no doubt Vine where is Davis."In the back on the phone sir,"King hello can you hear me,"Yes why are you whispering" "Im on the job your boy just sent motherfucker to the little guy baby momma's house killed her the kids and burned them and tried to burn the house down."Fuck you mean tried!"something went wrong and if they left anything behind that traces back to Just or themselves there done so protect yourself."Davis get the fuck off the phone! We working here."Yes boss.(click) "sorry sir that was my mom."I don't give a damn who it is the feds all on us we need to find something and im sure for them to want to burn shit down they left something behind."Ryder Janet Davis called she said that stupid mother fucker sent someone over they killed Lil Spade baby mom and kids and tried to burn the house down but it didn't burn."Dam King i told you this dude is reckless he living like this back in the day you do murders they come back on your ass the only people i know who would do some shit like that is the twins Cain an Abel and i never heard of them slippen up like this if they left anything behind the feds are gonna get them what should we do."I'm thinking i don't know if we should kill the twins they don't have any link to us but Just is pushing it im starting to lose respect for the old head matter fact let me call him and check his temperature.(ring,ring)"Yeah what's up?"Just im hearing things it's getting outta control and them people are in everyone's business."Look King i been very polite up to now i handle my shit how i do if you don't like it step up and do something or stat the fuck outta my shit im no fucking kid to report! (click)"Hello! hello, King hello!)"well fuck you to then,"What happend Just King hung up," Just you was talking to him aggressive ." Shut the fuck up Kamren!"Yo Just you outta pocket using my government name."Oh sorry is the baby hurt shut the fuck up Killa i run my shit how i run it do as you told or get left behind,"Yeah ok boss" "By the way boss King says it's no beef handle your shit how you see fit but from this moment on we won't do any business anymore."I don't give a fuck send him his money we owe i will find another connect after we off the young boy who needs King now i have all the reason in the world to crush his ass fuck the love the nigga is a seat warmer in my spot anyway i shoulda let them niggas kill his ass in prison anyway,Fuck you looking at me like im bugging for Killa?"You got it Just i didn't say a word it your play whatever however you wanna play it. "King i sent Killa the message he text back he told Just said if possible he would like to meet up later with me or you to discuss him grabbing for his own thing since Just trippin."It's on you what you think you trust it won't be a set up i mean i'm not going i trust your instinct but if it is a trap we both not getting caught out there."nah it's not a trap me and Killa been getting close since we the ones be meeting up for the exchanges he been telling me about Just is too wild and trippin."Yeah i hear you but a man that will switch up on a person rather they winning or losing will switch up on you."No King i don't think he would do that besides he told me he wouldn't turn on Just or give him up to anyone trying to harm him out of loyalty he said if anything he would pop his ass his self, it's he don't see that killen everything is bringing heat and gonna bring their downfall."I hear you do what you feel you're a boss too and your gonna run the show soon when i retire after i take care of Eddie and them cops."Aye Just i need to go check up on my girl," Ok cool take me cross town to the block so i can ride thru so niggas see my face and know im still here."You mean we still here."Oh that's right we still here." How long will you need with your girl we need to get on this young nigga asap."Not long an hour or two so i can let her know it's all good im alive and all."Ok cool let's go to the block."Grandma thanks for the food it was awesome."Ok Lil Spade you sure you don't want to stay a few days to relax i mean after everything thats happen boy i havn't see you greave or anything."Grandma im ok it is what it is besides i got a feeling everythings gonna be alright."Son you mean you have a feeling."Yes maam" Ok baby make sure you come back and see me soon i be so worried you out there running them streets like Ace used to."Ok grandma i have to go see you soon my ride outside."what's up auntie why didn't you want to come in and speak."You know why the old bag be trippen she can sense when a person is up to no good but any way what's good nephew? I got a line on them people i hear they on they block like it's nothing."Thanks auntie when i get this shit taken care of and i get back right i'm gonna bless you let's head over there."Davis,and Vine yes sir boss,"We are about to head to overtown i hear Just and his crew is over there i'm about to try a new tactic and confront him with what i got not everything but what i got so go get the car you two and i will be out front in 5 min let me get my gun out my desk."Ok boss!" Yo Vine that's the stupidest shit i ever heard you gone confront a career criminal that knows the law you won't get shit,Yeah Davis i think Johanasson is in over his head on this one."What did you say about me Vine? Oh nothing sir i said we need to head on over there now ,"Right so let's go before he leave i'm gonna make him sweat and you know what i may take his ass in for some questions lock him in to a story fuck you two looking like that for? " Do you have something you wanna say? "No sir" Ok then get to driving then." Aye Just we been here over an hour all

the youngins said the block still jumping but it's been hot ass hell the feds tried to plant some hidden cameras and some mics but our nighttime look outs got them shits and broken in pieces we got look outs on each corner and roof tops our only weak spot is the cleaners right here where we at we need to put men right here because of the alley."Yeah good work Killa get on that asap that way none of our young boys get caught slippin and make sure they strapped up or close by the straps at all time shit keeping it real since it's so hot this maybe the safest place only a dummy would come thru here and shoot shit up when cops always around.
(click,clack) "Or a nigga out for revenge don't move old head finally caught you slippen and you don't have heat im gonna enjoy this."Look here Lil nigga this my hood im never slippen if you shoot you won't make it out the block alive."See old head that's the difference between the youth and you old niggas who said anything about making it out your done this is for my unc and my men you killed now stop bitching it's time to die."screech.screech,"Dont fucking move F.B.I. put that fucking gun down your surrounded."Good thing me and you stayed and watch the block a little Vine before i ran in im glad you two finally told me your concerns and we called the rest of the team for back up they were getting a lil restless with having no action now look at this we got Lil Spade in custody for a weapon and Just and Killa for some routine questioning, Even though from what i see Lil Spade will make bail he don't have a record i want you to question him, I will question Just and Davis will question Killa,Lets head to the headquarters."Well,Well,Well,"Lil Spade we caught you with a gun."Hold up fed im not talking my 500 dollar an hour lawyer is already here so fuck you and fuck what you talking about,"knock,knock"Johansson this lil piece of shit high powered lawyer is here matter fact all they all are being released so wrap this up."ok cap give me 2 min."Ok Lil Spade you outta here but let me tell you this you won't win against Just, look at these photos look at your kids look at your woman he burned them!"you don't owe him anything fuck the street code tell me something, ok so you just gonna sit there you know what it's your funeral get your black ass outta here."Dam Just they let us all go at the same time why do you want to wait here we can't do anything to him in front of the fed building,"Killa i know but if you look over my shoulder to the left the twins are parked they gonna following him and snatch his ass up i told the young boy he won't go to the length of

violence i will go to any one that thinks there ahead of me im ten steps ahead of them it's chess not checkers."here he comes out the building Just."Well what's up old man them people saved your ass i was gonna blow your fucking head off now yo man Killa i don't have an issue with so if i was you i wouldn't fuck with this dude he's gonna fall! (ring,ring,) hello!"oh yeah ok pull up. (click) "Nice try old man you got your people sitting waiting to snatch me up god try but not today you see them cars coming down from the right and the left they with me and they strapped so if you don't want a bloodbath call of your hit squad."You got it Lil Spade but remember the next time we see each other it's gonna be violence."likewise old head" "Killa who the fuck is in them tintend out tahoe we killed all his men."I don't know who it is but i know who it's not it's not Crazy Eddie who we would suspect to help him and i know this because he is in hiding from King."Well whoever the fuck they are they gonna die i gave the twins the signal not here but to follow them and kill them all."welcome lil Spade that was a close call you know Just woulda killed you right there he don't give a fuck." yeah i can't lie until you called me i was trying to figure out how to get out the situation and it's fuck up the feds want us to kill each other so they can clean up the mess' but enough about that i see you reach out to me so what can i do to assist."Well the first thing i want you to do is watch the monitor as we pull up at the light you see that car follow us is his outta town hittas the twins they won't stop until they kill you so watch what we have in store for them."Aye Cain not so close we dont want them to see us and hand me the grenade launcher because i know that truck is probably tinted."Somethings off Able they turning on a street where everything's abandoned now we the only!"Hold up Cain what's that in that abandoned house hold up i think we surrounded. (peww,bang,bang,peww,) "Yo you got them niggas dam they shot all the fuck up good looking whatever you need you got it." I'm glad you said that i want your properties you own i want every piece of land then i want you to get out of town you are to lay low until my people pick you up here's the paperwork i drew up sign it and we good."Ok no problem long a you take care of Just ass but i can't stay gone for ong soon as i get me another team together i'm back."stop right here driver stop."Ok here's the spot lay low until we come from you."Ok cool and thanks again i never thought you would come to my aid being as though you knew i put them pigs on you but thank you for seeing thru the bullshit and letting it go i'll wait right here King!"Driver pull off."King that lil nigga happy as hell Just got the best of him if he stayed on the street any longer the feds would've got for good or Just woulda killed his ass, Now i understand why you helped him for the properties but that nigga tried to set us up before."Ryder don't even worry he won't live to long im making sure the paper work go thru them im gonna finish his ass myself then we will dispose of his body where no one will find him, im thinking at grinding factory we'll turn his ass into fertilizer."Ok King we got that mapped out now we gotta deal with Just bitch ass. (ring,ring)"hello,what,who,"what's up Just?"they found the twins dead who the fuck is strong enough to get to them and catch them slippen,"Killa find out so i can wipe they whole family out.

CHAPTER 10:
RYDER & KILLA

Yo Killa! What up son? "It's all good Ryder, let's get down to business. " Well you already know King not supplying Just anymore because the nigga don't have respect for anything he bringing heat to everyone and to be honest people are tired, not only us but there are other people higher on the ladder than King, the Judges we pay off the politicians, cops, pretty much everyone that has something to lose, all ya boy had to do was sit back collect money and ball out and die a rich old happy man, but no he has to prove his balls are bigger than everyone else and not for nothing i been wanting to crush his old ass but King got so much love and respect for the guy he been letting it slide I'm telling you Killa the guy is setting himself up for failure." Yo Ryder keeping it 100 i been trying to talk sense into the man but he do say King is his people and i do see he has some love for him but i think the jealousy or the power and money has gone to his head he thinks in his mind all this shit should be his and you and everyone else should be picking up work from him. It's like nothing i say or do gets to him and i fucks with Just for real but i see he is taking the crew down a lane to self-destruction." Speaking of your crew, how are they feeling right now? How do they see everything? Are they happy with the current situation? "No they are pissed but they are loyal they won't outright turn on him not for King or no one else, they see things as its war and that comes with the game but they feel he's going overboard especially with the kids you know our crew is mostly Haitians some were down with the Zoes back in the day so they are very superstitious and feel like killing the kids and

70

the baby mom was some fucked up shit and they are not happy. 'I would say that 90% of them would ride with me if I made a move. I think I could convince the rest if it made sense business wise. The thing is we were so loyal that we tried to talk to him, but the power and money had consumed him. " You know that's what King was thinking since you spoke on that he was like let's not give him anymore work get what's owed from him and cutoff all contact and let's see what he does," I mean we knew he would try to go around us and reach out to the Columbian, Mexicans, and the Cubans but they won't serve him at best he would have to get some work from the Dominicans with so much cut in it he wouldn't even be able to get that shit off after a while, 'Listen Killa Ima keep it 100 with ya Just is on a path to self-destruct if he don't switch up that old way of thinking it's gonna get him killed or life in prison and to be real with you i seen this coming a mile away these old heads can't let go of what they was or they get jealous of a young nigga getting it and thinking it should be them that's on top instead of being content with what they have, He's done and im not tryna convince you to do anything but i fuck's with you my nigga and i hate to see you get caught up in his b.s. "I feel you Ryder my only issue with pushing him out the way is my morals i live by the street code all thru my body you know the rules you pick a side and even if the side you pick is the losing one you go down with the ship, the only reason I'm considering this shit is because i know Just wrong and the nigga low key keep disrespecting me almost as if he' threatening my life, 'Word are you serious?" Yeah the nigga was wilding out the other day and i can't seem to get thru him he definitely feel like King, you, and everyone else is in his way if they don't go with his program he told me as much speaking like he will take me out if he has to, so for that reason alone he has to be stop, 'Oh you made up your mind" "Yeah sitting here thinking about the shit pissed me off let me know what you need me to do but i have to say I'm going to take over his shit i don't want to do this then King wants his turf'. Don't worry my nigga you got that King is about to retire after all loose ends are done i will be running the show and you my nigga so you got my word as bond the spot will be yours.'Ok Ryder I'm about to be out get at me if i don't answer text me I'm probably with Just but i have to be careful he be on everything moving."Ok ill holla later Killa" (ring, ring, ring,) "Hello!" "He's all in King." Ok come see me when you get done with whatever you are doing "Ok i will but if i don't get back up tonight tomorrow for sure. (ring, ring, ring,) "what's up Just? "Where the fuck you at? " On my way to the block why is everything ok? " No everything's not ok Lil spade is hiding and fuck all that get your black ass over here I'm on the block now."Ok Just I'm 10 min away.'Ok Ryder we have to flush the Lil Spade nigga outta hiding, i talked to some people that put me in contact with Crazy Eddie and he said fuck that lil nigga he was gonna killem anyway so do what i have to do, 'Hold up Just you talk to Eddie? Do you know where he is? so we can drop the info to King. 'Don't interrupt me again Killa and no i don't know where he at and if i did i wouldn't tell King shit."But Just King is your people man that's not how the game is to be played one hand washes the other remember. 'No fuck all that I'm changing the rules anyone not with us is against us so how you feel about my decision Killa?" I'm good. 'That's what I wanted to hear from your mouth from now on i do the thinking I'm the boss you take orders you're the soldier. 'Dam King did you here all that Killa recorded everything that fucking loudmouth traitor said and sent it to me now i know you're the boss. 'Hold up Ryder i don't need you saying anything push his fucking wig back bring his head to me on a silver platter, I feel like this shit my fault when i met the nigga in prison he showed me the ropes being as though i was new but sometimes i got the feeling he was trying to son me i can't believe the nerve of this old head mother fucker thinking he can fuck with me, but on another note it has to be planned carefully he's no slouch if he think you coming he killing everything in sight and i know you told his boy Killa you would let him have his hood but you better make sure you can trust that nigga."Say no more King im on his ass i feel like if he can turn on Just he might do us the same later down the line he talking about his morals earlier i thought to myself yeah but you willing to kill that nigga for us so don't you worry i got him we killing two birds with one stone. 'See Ryder that's how i Knew you was boss material. 'Thanks, King, for believing in a nigga when you retire, I'm gonna make you proud all your payments will be on time will i deal with the connect. 'No i will meet with him or we will email each other but everything else will be left in your hands." Ok King, what's next on the agenda today? 'we have to get rid of Lil Spade, i was thinking we kill em or drop a line to Just that would confuse his ass on why we helping him when we cut him off, " We also have to finish this thing with crazy Eddie before him and Just band together although i know

Just would still kill him to in the end." Yeah, King the old head is really tripping but i guess that's what power and money does." Yeah, Ryder but the problem is his old way of thinking is about to ruin him, 'Let's be out head to the spot." Aye Just everything is good out here on the block, but we will run outta work real soon. 'Killa i been trying to call the fucking Cubans, the Mexicans, and everybody else but no one will fuck with me or either they work is garbage." Maybe we should call King and talk all this small petty shit out Just before it gets outta hand." Fuck King i won't bow down to that ungrateful piece of shit i showed his ass the ropes and kept the wolves off his ass in prison brung that nigga into my thing and this the thanks i get fuck that nigga and the bitch who made him. 'Just! King got love for you his thing is his thing to run how he see fit i think, 'There you fucking go again what the fuck i tell you about thinking if you keep it up you won't be thinking nothing because your brains will be on the sidewalk now shut your scary ass up about King matter fact get of his dick and go hand out packs or something while the big boys play lil nigga."Ok Just,"whatever you say.

CHAPTER 11:
KINGDOM COME

Ryder head over to the safe house but drive the speed limit i got two guns in the stash box a mac and a Draco we gonna end this Lil Spade thing then focus on Eddie then Just." Ok King let's go." Let me see your phone Ryder so i can tell the Lil nigga be out ready when we pull up." King, we got a tail i can't tell who it is but i suspect it's Crazy Eddie or his boys by the car they driving." Yeah Ryder that BMW is fa sho Eddie and he's stupid enough to do the work his self, don't stress this truck is bullet proof even bomb proof so his ass will be in for a rude awaking let's lure him to the safe house let me call the young boy. (ring, ring, ring, ring,) What's up King." We on our way about 10 min from you go to the closet in your bedroom you will see about 15 guns pick some we got Eddie following us we gonna pull in to the gate when i hit my remote it will box him in and raise a wall you make sure you're on the balcony and light his ass up one more thing there's armor piercing bullets in the drawers in the closets' King doing it now."Yo Ryder change of plans we not gone kill the Lil nigga we putting him under the wing he ready to jump wherever we say just to get rid of all his enemies i think he will be loyal. 'King i agree i wanted to motion it but didn't want to overstep my boundaries, here we go King he's coming up fast. 'Hurry up get in the gate so i can box his dumb ass in."Mac! King is stupid ass fuck he don't even see us he must be getting close to his destination he's slowing down if he goes into any of these houses we gonna slaughter everyone in the house then I'm gonna send for my people from the ATL so we can take over everything that was his i think instead of killing his bitch i will keep her as my token of destroying her nigga,'Slow down Mac they pulling in that house soon as they get in the gate bum rush it and crash into they bumper, now!go!go! Screech , screech, clank,clank,"what the fuck Eddie we trapped in they set us up."Mac ram it in reverse, 'Oh shit who is that on the balcony? Unfucking believable it's Lil Spade he down with, blaaat,blaaat, blaaat, blaaat."Ryder look at the mother fucker squirm and jump around in the car Lil Spade is letting the SkS loose on they ass."Yeah he letting loose all the tire flat the car not moving but it looks to be bulletproof. 'Oh really give me the speaker control hit the button to take the car underground Lil spade this is King you can stop shooting meet me in the basement. 'Oh shit just they lowered us in the ground filled with water and crocodiles look there is King and Lil Spade and that must be Ryder." Ok Eddie you wanted this so you got it granted your protected by your car from bullets but not water so your options are get the fuck out the car hands up and face my wrath or stay in the car and drown, Ha, ha, ha, ha ,ha "Eddie how the fuck we getting outta this one ?" Mac we not we either get out and die or stay in and die, I'm not going out like no coward Ima face this nigga ,"No Eddie don't I'm staying. 'See you in hell my friend, Ok King I'm stepping out. 'Hands in the fucking air and stand on the wood deck right there it will lift you up, 'Oh your boy not getting out your gonna love this watch what happens," Lil Spade hit the button right there.' thump ,boom, 'King don't kill my man can't we work something out. 'Don't beg you look weak you pose to be Crazy remember Eddie you gone kill my woman and your cousin, 'Now watch you see the water disables the electric system which unlocks the doors and right about now your boy is about to get out in the water for fear of drowning now comes the moment of truth.

Growl, clamp clamp, "Aggh, aghh help! Eddie, help! They are eating me alive to help! 'Look Eddie when you fuck with the King you get the Kingdome the crocs ate your man alive now as for you get your bitch ass thru these doors tie his ass up Spade and put those cuffs on his legs and hands to make sure he is secured to that chair. 'King listen." Oh now you wanna talk let's be clear you gonna die today you came here to kill me my woman and your cousin but mostly my woman so fuck all the talking and copping please be a man and die like the gangsta you claim to be. 'King look please i will leave here you won't see me again in life i have 40 million dollars saved i will give you that please King. 'Stop this

nigga from talking here Lil Spade cut his fucking tongue out. "
Please Spade don't do this ."Fuck you old head i helped you and you
was gonna kill me i picked the wrong side King is a real ass nigga
he could have killed me for that b.s. But instead he helped me and
showed me the error in my ways and for that I'm loyal to him until
death now open your fucking mouth, (agrrrgh, arghhh,) "Now you
bitch ass nigga talk with out your tongue, King what you want me
to do with it? "Throw it to the crocs, 'Now Eddie, I'm gonna sit here
while you get punished for your disrespect. (mmmm,mmmm) "I
can't hear you speak up ha-ha! Ha! " Hey hand me the bat Ryder.
'King i like this kid here you go Lil Spade."Crack,whomp!" Owwl,
you broke my knee caps please stop I'm begging you please." Shut
the fuck up! You thought you were gonna kill me? "Crack,
whomp!"Look at your fucking head? 'Enough! Lil Spade kicked his
chair over in the croc pool now."Ok King, 'Good by Crazy Eddie,
(thud,) "aghh,help!crack,mmm,crack," Dam King i never saw a
man get ate alive by crocs before thanks for the experience, and
thanks for killing this m.f. You have every right to kill me for
telling him your spots and whereabouts and i won't run or bitch
out but if you spare me i promise to be loyal to you but if not i
accept my fate." I like you Lil nigga and after talking it over earlier
with Ryder we decided you can be valuable so we want you on the
team, and your first order of business is to Kill Just he is no longer
family Ryder and me and the whole team are on his ass but be
aware he will not be easy to get rid of he will go to a lengths you
may not be willing to do but we have one element of surprise he
doesn't know we're teaming up and he doesn't know we have an
inside man so bottom line is we need to strike first and strike hard,
'but first order of business Ryder call the girls up so i can tell them
we almost done here. (ring, ring,) Hello! Destiny it's done you and
Cherry are safe but me and Ryder have a few more loose ends to tie
up so to be sure we need you to stay put a lil while longer. Ok King
we was wondering when we was going to hear from you I'm
staying put i love you so much baby and i miss you and i know
Cherry miss Ryder." I love you to babe speaking of Cherry, put her
on the phone please so Ryder can speak with her i will speak to you
again real soon ok. Ok babe! "Cherry the Phone! 'Hello!" Hello babe
me and King took care of everything you two are good after we
take care of a few things we will pick you up so still take
precautions and be safe. Ok babe we will i love you and I'm sorry
about everything. 'No need to say that what's understood don't

need to be said love you and i will talk to you later. (click) "King they seem in good spirits under the circumstances." Yeah, they do but let's get back to work aye yo Lil Spade come here! 'Yeah, what's up King. " How much of your team is intact still. 'King that son of a bitch killed them all in the warehouse then killed my baby mother and kids and this nigga killed my Unk he in the wrong for all this shit and if i can get my hands on his ass it's over for that old nigga."Relax you will get your chance i came up with a plan but trust me it won't be easy, and it's no guarantee it's for sure life or death Just is no one to be taking lightly and on the real i got love for the old head but he'outta pocket and has to be dealt with because if not he will be a problem for everyone in the future so we gone have to use all resources on his ass."King he killed all my men with them crazy ass twins that you got dealt with it's no telling what else his crazy ass will do an as you see he didn't give a fuck about you he knew where Eddie was and didn't say shit he was hoping you niggas kill each other so he could take over and what about his right hand man Killa that m.f. Is also dangerous as they come i done heard stories about him so I'm not too sure you can trust him. 'Trust we don't trust him me and King already peeped his snake ways we had a gps tracker put on all his cars and anywhere they be but this thing is a delicate situation because all parties involved know the other moves and not to mention the feds are in town and they on everything don't think because they been quiet or they haven't made any arrest they not on it because they are. 'And Ryder don't forget my inside source tells me when the F.E.D. about to make a move so we have to be really careful my nigga I'm not blinded by any loyalty i had for old boy i know he's the enemy and we have to eradicate all threats to the throne." So, King being as though I'm new to the fold and i know u don't completely trust me what do you need me to do. 'It's not about trust much as proving yourself to the team and when i semi retire Ryder will be calling all shots so he will have to trust you also. 'Ryder! "I'm ready whatever you need me to do." That's what i like to hear lil nigga we gonna crush Just ass once and for all but we taking baby steps that nigga is ruthless for real so we have to be just as ruthless 'pun intended' "OK Ryder!, Lil Spade lets go over some things so we can figure out how to hit his ass where it hurts. 'Destiny! "Yes cherry," I will be glad when all this is over i thought it would end with my cousin Eddie but it's continuing with this guy Just, I'm so tired of the lifestyle and Ryder supposed to be taken over for King as he semi retires." Yeah girl i know what you mean i been on King's ass since he been home about getting out the game before it's too late we have money businesses and everything now he is retiring but still in it at the same time because he still has to meet the connects or at least put the deals together he still will be running things but won't be running the day to day i guess that's where Ryder comes in but i don't blame you for Tryna convince Ryder to stop.

CHAPTER 12:
DESTINY CALLS

Knock!knock!Knock! "Anyone home? Hello."Oh shit Cherry get your gun and open the panic room door."What's going on? Who is that at the door Destiny? It's Just and a few men with him if he comes thru this door this Ak will split they fucking head open!"I'm calling Ryder and King (ring, ring, ring) "What's up babe? Me and Destiny have our guns cocked back and ready with the panic room door open Just and his men are knocking on the door."What the fuck? We on the way if they come thru the door let they ass have it look at the cameras make sure there are no more men out there."There aren't any other men except for the 2 other ones with him but from the look of it he's not sure he's in the right place because he sees the place has a for sale sign so he really is looking around how did he find us." Babe we 5 min out get off the phone and watch your back Destiny." What the fuck Ryder how did he find out where they at."King the only one knew where they was at was me and you oh shit! The real estate agent im gonna kill that motherfucker,"No need bro if i know Just he killed her already we're here and it looks like the girls have they ass running Destiny shooting at them with the Ak(blattt, blattt, blattt,) " Hook left King i got a shot (boom, boom, boom,) I dropped one of the goons run that one ass over(screech,) " Ryder he ran thru the woods we don't have time we have to get the girls before the police come."They right there (screech)Destiny do you have everything ? Yes David hit the button Ryder blow the shit. (boom,boom) "What the hell Ryder we was in a time bomb this whole time and how the fuck did anyone know where we stay? "

babe it was the real estate agent. We didn't kill the mother fucker off because we didn't have time but we also didn't know we would be beefing with Just."Wait King what the hell? Destiny he snapped the power done got to him so it's war im sorry baby but im glad what we taught you protected you, the other safe house only me and Ryder know about." So you wanna stick us somewhere again how we know we safe Ryder." Babe you will be safe. I promise that shit back there was a fluke we didn't know," Just" would look into anything being as though he were people. 'Ok girls here is the new safe house see how its an hour 45min away from town no one will never no where this place is i bought this place before i went to prison so i had it for a min the other place wasn't mine the real estate agent gave us one of her places."Good thing it wasn't one of our places King because if someone saw me blowing that shit up it woulda traced backed to us and we already have the F.E.D.S., snooping around and now this hot as nigga want to go to war."See Ryder thats how you know a smart nigga from a stupid nigga, a get money nigga from an old washed up old head, if the nigga had any since he would chill the fuck out until them people lose intrest but no! " He gotta prove he got the biggest balls, but anyway fuck that nigga girls we staying here with yall tonight then in the morning we on that nigga head we leaving the bentley truck and taking the porsche truck it's faster we gone need it."Yeah King we gone need that shit but old boy he gone need all the support he can gett which won't be much only his men is in his corner no one else will dare come up against us i got the team all ready searching the city for his ass for the disrespectful shit coming after our ladies matter fact King we need to play that nigga game ." I know Ryder, I've been thinking the same but the problem is I don't think he has family or a girl but look check this out lets get some rest and we can talk about this shit in the a.m. "Just why? King is a good person and you attack his woman. Come on, even you know that's against everything. What are you doing? "Killa, Killa, Killa by the way you on King dick why would he need his bitch i thought i told you little man not to question my orders."Just i would do anything for us but you are outta control im begging you to, (aghhh, smack) "Shut the fuck up before i slap your bitch ass again matter of fact im tired of this game you playing you're playing both sides and im done." Just am I not supposed to be your second in command and give you advice and I feel this is wrong. I'm voicing my opinion but if you don't want me to, I won't say anything. I will go along with whatever you say." I will tell your ass again and if i have to repeat it again you wont live to even regret it .Im the fucking boss i run the fucking show do what you told or walk the fuck away before you not able to walk away at all i won't say this again next time off with your fucking head now get the fuck out my face and go make sure the money is right i have to meet up with my new connect tonight and i don't want anything short."Ok Just im on it." Aye Ryder let's be out did you tell the crew to meet at the spot i wanna get on this nigga." Yeah King they are waiting on us now before we have to stop in the beans neighborhood Killa wanna holla at us. I got Lil Spade down there already checking shit out making sure it's no setup."Destiny we out see you two later you're safe here. "Ok babe see you later."Cherry i love you babe see you later."Ok Baby love you to."Come on we taking the Jeep cherokee sport it's for situations like war it's fast and it's low key im driving today ryder."Cool King do ya thang. (vroom, vroom,) What i tell you fast as hell there go Killa right there lets pull up and get out."What's good? "King this nigga slapped the shit outta me in front of the whole crew i was gonna off his ass right there but i knew i wouldn't make it out alive he's obsessed he can't see that he's going down hill talking about killing you your team your girl and Ryder his girl and his whole family i told him i was gonna check out the block but dipped over here i think im gonna lay low until this shit is over then come and lay my shit down with a whole new crew." Killa i feel for you i knew Just was over the top but trust when i tell you this his days are numbered he's done he won't make it and his crew those that don't die with him will have the option to get down or get the fuck outta town. Ryder is there anyway i can stay at a safe house or any hotel you guys own out the way. " Take these keys room 210 in the hyatt it's in Edgewater but let me warn you once you do this Just will kill everything you love so don't' come back until this is over."Thanks King,Ryder i won't forget this when you bring me inside the team i will be your greatest asset i will ride for real that's my word is bond." I hear you so go to the hotel, lay low, don't tell anyone where u are and we will get back to you when this is all settled. "Aye King he maybe an asset if he feels loyal to us i think Just slapping him and he know the nigga unpredictable must have gotten under his skin to the point he's like fuck it." Yeah you Right Ryder it's a good thing he left when he did because if not Just was sure as hell gonna kill him sooner than later, i don't know what the fuck happen he was a diffrent o.g., In prison now its like he forgot how tight we were." I here you King but it is what it is we gotta do what we gotta do and that old nigga think all that crazy shit he be doing is gonna save him but it won't his time is over he's done." Yeah you're right he was my people in the pen but after trying to kill the girls it's kill or be killed so let's wrap his ass up. Hey pull over right here and tell the boy Spade to come out.(ring, ring, ring,) "Yo what's good Ryder ? Come on down we got some work for you," Ok on my way? "Ok king he is coming down."When he gets here we gonna break it down to him but we not mentioning Killa just in case we have to get rid of one or both these mother fuckers." Ok King cool oh here he is."What's up King,Ryder what are we getting into? "It's like me and King was saying the other day we want you to get rid of Just here are some address and some numbers to places he be at or chill at sometimes if u need any of the haitian mob help they on standby at the last place on the list circled, "Ok we dropping you off here that 88' box cutlass with the brown rag has the keys in it for you. "Thanks King this is a perfect under car to get at them niggas i'll holla at u when it's finished. "Ok Lil Spade ,pull off Ryder."That Lil nigga is trying his best to prove his gratefulness King."Yeah he is im still not sure what to do with him in the end but fuck all that did you sweep this car for bugs we have to assume them people is bugging everything,"Yeah i did everytime we pull in or pull out a garage in another car i do and sometimes i check when i get a funny feeling."Ryder we havn't seen or heard from the F.E.D.S. but that shit doesn't mean they are not around snooping but as a precaution i have signal blockers in my inside person with the F.E.D.S. gave me what they use but you know them people making new technology everyday, speaking of the devil she is texting me some shit now. Ok bet she said they got a line on Just so be careful they all over him they tried to bug our shit and find our women but they don't have a clue,"let me forward this shit to Lil Spade so he can stay on point,(send,bleep) "There the lil nigga should get it any minute."Oh shit King texting me right when im watching Just ass, what the fuck the feds are watching shit let me make sure none of these people are them before i try to blow his fucking head off. "Davis,Vine this roof top was a brilliant idea we can see everything from here i can see right into the building they have guns and everything in there Just must be preparing to hit someone"Sir you want me to call it in.?"Are you fucking crazy Vine we call it in now on some bullshit gun charges his people may say all the guns belong to them and Just ass will walk no we gonna watch him, i see that cutlass is pulling off i thought that was one of his people doing patrol but i guess not.(ring, ring) "I had a line on him but i'm pulling off i see them people on the rooftops."Ok be easy holla at me when you got a better position."Ryder they on the rooftop Lil Spades leaving now."Yo King maybe we should step back while they take his ass so we don't be in the mix or the Lil nigga don't be in the mix and fuck around and get jammed up." No i'm not backing down if he do get caught up or even if Just decides to say something to get out my inside man gonna hit his ass and anyone else needing to go,"Dam King you connected like a motherfucker,"Correction we connected you bout to run the whole shit."Yeah speaking of that my girl keep bugging me about stepping back when you do she has text me 15 times today about the shit i had to tell her stop i'm in the field and don't need any distractions." Look Ryder it's up to you if you wanna step off let me know i can make some other moves put another person in charge or better yet you don't have to run the day to day im meeting with the connect you can oversee the money and let one of the mob handle the street shit."Yo King that's what's up i like that idea let me tell her so she can back off. "What are you smiling at Cherry? "Ryder's giving me what i want see he loves me he text me King and him came up with he will just handle the money and not the street shit."See Cherry i told you power of the pussy gets them everytime .(a,ha,ha,) "Girl you crazy! "But you are right so since the boys are gonna be in semi retirement it looks like we need to make some plans to keep them busy we don't want them getting bored, "Yeah girl let's come up with some things i agree Destiny because i don't want either one of them in the streets no more. Johansson there is Just coming out the building now he has 6 bodyguards what the hell is he doing,"Vine it looks like he's looking around like he knows something up or he knows he's being watched." Maybe it's because he's at war and he's being careful. (bleep,bleep,) davis is calling on the two way hold up Vine keep on watching them,Yeah talk Davis, " Johansson somethings up he has binoculars and what appears to be a detonator or something in his hand im not sure but he may be on to use i think we should pull back Look! He's   staring up at you all now."Davis are you fucking crazy that piece of shit is crazy but he's not stupid. (boom, boom, boom,) Johansson! Johansson! (boom, boom, boom,) oh shit ! "Let's see them bug my shit now stupid ass feds think they smarter than me die! Mother fucker ! "Did you get them plates who the fuck was in that cutlass and where the fuck is Killa let]s be out before this place is swarming with them people. "Wow boss you got them motherfuckers your smart as hell you said they was following you and you was fucking right how did you know."

Tank, I knew it was either King or the F.E.D.S.but i was leaning more toward them people because i don't think King built like that and he's blinded by his respect and love for me but as for me this is business so when i kill him and everything he cares about he still will be my nigga he just will be a dead nigga, (ha, ha, ha, ha,).

"Hello King speaking, what he did fucking what are you kidding me i need to get there are you ok don't you worry that mother fucker gonna pay im not, what calm down this nigga almost killed you ok, ok, i want come down but keep me informed and if possible leave him on the streets ok got you later." King what the fuck did that nigga do? Ryder he blew the feds up that was on the roof he killed Johanasson he killed his team up there and my person that's on the inside ran from where she was from but he blew that up to she's hurt but says she will be ok, "King that nigga has to go how the fuck did he know."Listen Ryder it's possible to spot a tail but all this other shit he getting from someone and i know we set a fucking meeting up with them cops at the house the crocs should be hungry again and tell them park 3 blocks away and walk in it's time to end all this bullshit, but not all is bad they just put my inside person in charge of the bring Just ass down they know he was there but they have to prove he set the bombs off, but i told her to stall so i can get him she said she will try but they just called down 50 fucking F.E.D.S. to hit the city. "King, you know when they finish him or we finish him they coming for us! "Don't worry about that my inside person won't let that happen she already on it." Im more worried about this unpredictable nigga with his rage at lust for power and my down fall it's no telling what he would say or do if them mu fuckers caught him bitch ass nigga is outta control we not going to see the girls anymore until this is done we can't take anymore risk. " I agree I will text them we need to talk to Lil Spade," Yeah we do get him on the phone and explain to him. (ring,ring,ring) "What's up Ryder ? "Just killed some F.E.D.S. on the roof of the building you was at this nigga is smart he may know what you driving you may want to take the car to the spot and get another one." Yeah you may be right I felt someone was watching me. I wasn't sure if it was them people or

Just people but I'm ahead of you. I'm heading to one of the car locations now to swap out this car for another one. (blatt,blatt,blatt). "Yo what the hell? Lil Spade! Spade!.(click)." King, the phone went dead i think i heard shots im not sure." That fucking Just he may have killed the Lil nigga i guess we'll know if he calls back or not damn im sick of this nigga i thought the whole mob supposed to be after him what the fuck is up Ryder ? "Yeah the mob wasn't having any luck and as you know Just is no push over he bout that action. We have to come up with something or he will kill us off, and all our family and people. "Ryder this needs our full attention im sick of the B.S. and this nigga Just thinks he live and bout that action but it's time to turn the tables on his ass from this moment on send out the text the gloves are off we do whatever is necessary to bring this to an end, and i mean whatever,"Ok King it's done lets keep our bulletproof vest on," Ryder we can wear them but truth be told they won't be aiming for our vest they will be throwing head shots, but i can tell you one thing for sure the level of savagery we about to inflict on him and his people he won't see coming because he thinks im blinded by my respect for him but it's a wrap for that whole team." Im fucking tired of playing nice with his bitch ass it's a green light on every one that's associated with him." King it's fucking time you said that let's be out and handle this shit. " Aye yo Just that car that was at the spot wasn't the F.E.D.S. so i'm thinking it was King's people or some other crew but either way we on it what you want us to do they watching the guy now." Spider that's a dumb ass question and stop fucking thinking, leave that to me now hit the car and kill everything in it asap, "Ya dig.?" Ok cool we on it." Dam now which block did king say the other safe cars was on i got to get that shit then go back find Just and eliminate his ass to show Ryder and King im down wit em, who the fuck is this, sir can u move im tryna pull out,(blatt, blatt,blatt,) "Oh shit" screech,boom," ha,ha,ha, "lame ass non shooting mu fuckers you know who the fuck i am look at them in the dust, (ring,ring,) "What's up lil homie? "Yo them niggas found me some way probably followed me from the spot they was at they pulled up on me blocked me in but i crashed into they shit from the side and they airbag popped out, only thing they did is really make me wanna kill that nigga but i see he slick for real." Yeah he on one for sure be safe out there and handle your businesses."Yo Ryder they tried to hit Lil Spade but they didn't know the lil nigga was a hell of a driver,"Wow King

Just squad made a mistake somebody gonna pay for that shit cause just don't play with making mistakes. "Which one of you stupid mu'fuckers let that fucking driver escape a driver and 2 shooters and he still got away, dont all fucking speak at once. "Boss we blocked him in and he, (blam, blam,) "Next, be careful what you say or your brains will be leaking out like his matter fact (blam,blam,blam,blam) " Somebody clean this shit up and the next mu'fucker who makes a mistake might as well don't come back, because i will wipe out your whole bloodline kids and all and find that fucking traitor Killa i want his fucking head do you fucking here me.? " Yes sir boss" "Good now get the fuck outta my site before i kill you all," I want King fucking dead i want his woman dead i want Ryder dead and everything they love dead and if you pieces of shit can't do it i'll fly in some MS-13 killers and they will happily kill every nigga moving even you fucks. " King you think you will win your in over your head fuck nigga i will kill everything you love and then kill you last i will kill your second in command in a fucked up way." Boss, who are you talking to in here you ok? " I'm thinking out loud you dumb fuck now get the fuck in the streets and kill all our enemies before i kill you dumb ass. "Ok boss im out." "King you haven't seen the best of me yet im gonna destroy you and take the whole fucking city no the whole fucking state hostage every one will bow down to Just i will burn this bitch to the ground my next move will be my best move. (ha, ha, ha, ha,) "King I was thinking maybe we should reach out for a peace treaty at least until the F.E.D.S. leave town, what you think about that ? he will see it as a weakness and still try to crush us sooner or later i don't think you understand, we was in the pen and caught a beef with some spanish nigga the gaurd came in an broke that shit up lock us down so for two months while on lock he was plotting his next move, so one day he goes to the shower with like 6 of his goons the guards come in and do count they like where the fuck is everyone so they check the whole dorm first before even thinking about hitting the alarm, "what a fucking mistake that was" so they get to the shower and go in when they go in they get slaughtered, and the kicker is they cut they heads off and somehow get the machete they used and the heads out the prison, but they wasnt even done at the same time his other people burned all the spanish dudes up in they cell with some gasoline they snuck in , the warden and the other guards figured the heads were burt up with the rest of the bodies but they was so wrong, man thats the reason they turned the whole prison int a 23 hour lock down facility.

CHAPTER 13: DEATH COMES EASY

Ok team we all know who the target is the name is Just he goes by names like Just in credible, aka Just about anything he's a slick drug kingpin know for killing there is no limit on what he would do he went to prison around 20 some years ago we thought that was the end he was in there for killing a man then burning and pissing on the man after he was dead. Now most people when they get another chance at freedom would chill out but not Just he came home and hit the ground rolling Mr. Justin Clark as he's called in the legal system is a modern day terrorist that has no respect for law enforcement citizens or anyone he's suspected of even killing his dad when he was 12 for punish him for bad behavior his dad was found in bed with his throat slit there was no force entry and only him and his dad was in the house he later went to live with his mom where he was known in here neighborhood to bully other kids and harm animals he was so persuasive that he convince the kids in the neighborhood to get down and he form his first street gang his mom didn't like the direction he was going in she scolded him, and in typical Just way he slapped his mom and terrorize her for months until she escape from a second floor window and called the cops. The judge instead of giving a young Just time sentence him to community service and it was mandatory he see a therapist. The therapist declared him psychotic, delusional, and a narcissist , she also prescribed him a variety of pills to control his behavior and how did he thank her. He allegedly ran her over with a stolen car , it was alleged because all the witnesses that saw what happen disappeared and it was 6 total people that ended up dead so after they release him with no proof he went back home and his mom was gone she was such in fear of her life that she abandoned him at that time he was around 14 years old and every since then he been taking care of himself . Now team i say all that to say this Detective Johansson and a whole team of agents deputized by the bureau was killed, i was there outside in another building and i felt something was wrong so i left out the building and at that moment the building blew up and threw me into some parked cars and almost knocked me out, i look up to the roof and saw the roof blow up i saw Detective Johansson head explode off his body like a fucking watermelon, this fucking guy killed my boss and my whole fucking team, now with that said are there any questions.? "Yes you in the blue tie, what's your name ? and what's your question? " Hello my name is Ted doorman my question is how can we assume it was him but have no proof just because we were surveilling him so how can we say that he did it for sure.? " Ok Ted is it you can tell you're a fucking rookie we're the F.E.D.S. we know it all we have a 95 percent conviction rate if we say you guilty then you are we are the elite and i don't like you or what you're alluding to, you're fired get the fuck out and take your bitch ass back to basic training you fucking peon. " But let me explain what i mean." Get the fuck out before your done for good and don't (bam) "Slam the fucking door, bitch ass slam it anyway are there any more question? No good, now take your ass in the field. I have to make a phone call. (ring, ring, ring,) "Hello, "Yes what's up? " Did you get the fax I sent? "Yes, it came in 3 min ago. What's good? I sent my team out to hunt his ass down, the nigga is crazy he killed his dad killed his therapist and his mom hide from him and we think even she is dead this fucking guy is really nuts he has no family, no woman he fucks hoes so he doesn't have to commit to anyone he really is a dangerous man and to keep it 100 he loves this drama shit but we having some problems on our end to with this case. "What are the issues you're having? " We don't have any evidence that he has blown up the building and it's hard to put anything on him because the case is high profile and the fucking director is watching us very close." Look let me explain something to you we don't want him picked up we want him dead so when you know his moves you text this burner and we gone handle the rest and keep them mother fuckers off my back because when he dies i know they may target me next." Ok King I will send you any and all info on his whereabouts but i want double my pay for this it's very risky." Ok say less holla." (click) " What's up King everything ok .? " My contact just sent me info on Just it's over there beside the fax machine." Dam King from reading this shit the nigga is more crazier than i thought he killed his dad and a fucking shrink and his mom supposed to have left because she was afraid of what he would do for committing him to the psyche ward, he probably killed her from the looks of this info damn what the fuck ? " Ryder we gonna have to get deep on this shit this nigga don't seem to have any weakness even in jail no one came to see him or wrote any letters but it's one thing for sure that i learned from his old ass is everyone has a weak spot its up to us to find what it is. "Now it's on i have to find Just bet his ass is at that warehouse cross town i will soon find out in a few seconds, What the fuck we have here guys leaving the warehouse this fool maybe actually in here, let me check my gun ,clip, back up clip and silencer ,yeah I'm good to go now to sneak in you gonna learn today old man do fuck with Lil Spade, no one seems to be in here wait i here talking coming from that office in the corner, (click, clack) " Put your fucking hands in the air Just i got your mu' fucking ass now you bitch ass nigga you killed my uncle you killed my family you are going to die today you dumb fucking nigga, and what the fuck you smiling and laughing at (ha, ha, ha,) " I'm smiling because i knew one of you dumb fucks would come here thinking i was slipping I'm laughing because you wont get to pull the trigger don't you see the red beams on your head, (clunk, clunk) " Dam Killa you knocked his ass out cold. " Yeah look at his ass and I bet when we torture his ass he will admit he is down with King and he will give us a location on all his shit and maybe them bitches too. " The best thing you did Killa did was make King think you betrayed me hell even i thought you did." Never Just, that's why i came up with the plan i knew if i did King would kill me later now his dumb ass think im down with him so all we gotta do is get his ass to come to me at the safe house and end this shit." Yeah in due time but first wake this nigga up so i can put him back to sleep for ever (ha, ha, ha, ha,) "(slap, slap, slap slap,) " Wake up sunshine, "Look Just you got me," kill me and get it over with." Oh in due time now tell us where King is hiding out at matter fact grab his phone put it on video mode and call them niggas (ring, ring, ring,) Yo King it's Lil Spade, answer it Yo what's up lil nigga, Yo they got me Just and Ki...(clump,) shut yo bitch as up look at him knocked out wake him up," Well, Well ,Well, King you keep losing my brother your not smarter than me stop tryna get people to turn on me stop Tryna, (click) I'm glad you hung up on him he talks to much throw the phone out the window." King he said stop Tryna get people to turn on him like he knew something was up." he does Ryder i told you no more underestimating him Lil spade will die but that nigga Killa haven't been answering the phone turn on the tracker we put on his coat ," hey King according to the tracker his last movement was moving fast toward the projects, in Just hood then it stopped moving 4 blocks before like he's at a stand still for 10 hours or something." Nah my nigga he not at a fucking stand still and there is no way a nigga that's worried about that crazy ass nigga Just would go near him so either he Tryna line us up for the nigga or he's up to some other shit but either way somethings off call old girl that we had watching the place and see what she says real quick. "Hey King she said he been in and out everyday and she saw some cars passing by like they was watching him but they didn't stop like they knew or thought someone was watching but what made her think he was cool with the guy's in the car was his mannerisms when the car passed he nodded his head to them. 'Ryder did she say what kind of car it was. 'Yeah!" "It was a 4 door amg gray big body Benz." We gottem that was Just he love them fucking cars Killa must have had a change of heart or it was the plan all along either way we gone slaughter his ass, so if he calls for any type of meet we know to set up on his ass i told you he couldn't be trusted homie." Yeah King you was on point with that shit i feel bad for Lil Spade they gonna torture his ass to the death but the lil homie knew what was up if he got caught up i know what thing for sure i want to make Just ass suffer like he has done to so many other niggas life's he has affected. " Don't trip Ryder, his day is coming sooner than he thinks and he doesn't know we figured out Killa is really with him so let's put this plan into action so when Killa calls we will be ready to crush their ass. (arghh, help, aghh,) " Screaming wont help lil nigga you picked the wrong side why don't you tell me what King is planning and where he's hiding at and i will make death come easy for you, they gonna die anyway they don't know Killa is still down with me so make it easier on yourself. Fuck you Just you bitch ass nigga! i will never tell you shit so bring on whatever pain you want I'm built for it hoe ass nigga." Oh really well let's see how tough you are when you're castrated, and i know your illiterate ass don't know what that is so i will explain it to you it's when Killa here pulls down your clothes and cut off your balls with those big ass shears in his hands snip, snip, (ha, ha, ha, ha)n" Yeah where is all the tough guy shit now, Killa get it done. " With pleasure boss let me bull this down, oh shit the lil nigga pissed and shitted all over his self but look at this you're gonna bleed to death lil nigga tell us what's Kings plan, your being too stubborn you have no balls and Yous a bitch, no really now Yous a bitch Killa I'm tired of this game he's not gonna talk shoot his ass in both knee caps. (bang, bang, bang) "Dam Just the 40 Cal knocked off both his knees son is finished. " Well Lil Spade or lil shit whatever the fuck you are or was your good as dead now I'm gonna leave you hear to bleed to death so you can slowly suffer, matter fact give me the gun Killa, well lil shit i think i will kill you after all because you may not die right away and i wouldn't want them feds to find you but before you die i want you to know I'm gonna find the rest of your family you got in town and well you know the rest. (bang,bang,bang) "Well Killa another one down ,once we find King and kill the head the body will die now get rid of this body he's fucking disgusting and let's find them two niggas King and Ryder and end this bullshit. " Ok, I'm taking the body to the landfill. I will be back in 25 min then we can go on the hunt. Can you help me lift him in the bed of the truck? Ok come on 1, 2, 3, swing him(swish) thud," Dam he hit the back of the flat bed hard as hell , I'm out Just i will be back in 25. "Ms. Davis we have a line on one Mr. Justin Clark we have been on an associate of his phone named Killa B a.k.a. Killa b.k.a. As Kamren Cook we got a tail on him and we believe he has drugs and or guns in a blue f-150 pick up truck he's in but the issue is we don't have any probable cause so i have the team following him to see where he is going with whatever he has on him or in the truck also here is the address on this paperwork where we think Just is. Good job very good job Pikes i knew you would be an asset but remember we have to play this by the book we can not have any legal issues everything has to be clean Mr. Clark has 1000 dollar an hour lawyers on his payroll and if we was to stop Mr. Cook his lawyers would get him out asap or either he would die asap it depends on how Mr. Clark matter fact don't even call him mister call him Just he doesn't get the respect to be called mister or sir he's a fucking animal that killed over 10 police on that roof top and even though we know that piece of shit did it we have nothing no witnesses no fucking proof Just our police instincts but you mark my fucking words Pikes he will get what's coming to him rather it's a bullet or a cell he will get his now on that note is there anything else you would like to discuss. " Yes Ms. Davis we have been trying to follow King we have put bugs in places and undercovers on the street but it seems like he's always one step ahead i think he has someone in law enforcement on his payroll because it's no. (stop) "Excuse me ma'am." Let me stop you, this investigation is no longer focused on King. It's Just he is doing all the killing and all the torture King has been laying low now if he comes out doing the same bullshit we will revisit this conversation until then focus all manpower on Just that's an order understood? (yes ma'am). Ok now get out i have a headache and i need to make a call (ring,ring,ring,) King its that double o number again u want me to answer it? No, pass me the phone hello, Ok i see alright got it holla at me later i will call from a new phone next time. Hey Ryder go across town to Biscayne Blvd. Just is supposed to be holed up there but don't pull up on the block because the feds supposed to be watching but if they pick up Killa at where he's at Just may get away then we will follow the feds is next door watching so we gonna go across the street i know the owner so we should be good with watching how things play out. King if they get Killa i highly doubt if he lives Just won't take a chance on him ratting he don't trust no one." If he dies fuck him he had a chance to be on the winning team but he thought he was smarter than us i hope he don't even get caught so my contact can tell me where he at and we get to him first. Ok King there is the warehouse across the street we're gonna park over here and if we go in this building we should be able to see everything as long as no f.e.d.s. Are in here to come on let's go up to the roof. "Hold up I'm right behind you Ryder let me get the binoculars out the trunk (bam) dam my fault didn't mean to slam the trunk let's go, dam that was the longest 8 stories ever man when we done with offing this nigga i may half to workout something with you on that Ryder and King, " hey King look on the third floor of the building across the street you'll see some movement but i cant make out if it's Just or not. Yeah i see it and it is Just i can tell by the nigga walk he's a cocky mu' fucker but if you look to the other building across from that you will see them people looking right at his ass and from the looks of things they all over the front I'm glad we came in from the back way or they would have for sho seen us and i don't know if my FBI contact could've gotten us off of any surveillance footage let's get up outta here we can't get the nigga from here but if we had a dam 30 r 6 with the scope on it we coulda pick his ass off from here but i don't think that would've satisfied me i wanna look in that nigga eyes and let'em know its's me King killing his ass nigga, but that nigga Just so stubborn he's gonna be defiant until the end but make no mistake life will be better when he's out the picture and we taking over all his spots and any workers we feel that won't get down, we kill off and that way we take over all his spots that should be another 20 million or so a month i may even up our kilo count to a ton a month on cocaine and another ton on the heroin we would clear an easy billion after expenses that means everyone get's a bump in pay you get a double bump Ryder because of your loyalty and when you take over its points off every kilo you should clear 2 million a month yourself. 'Dam King good fucking looking out that's what the fuck I'm talking about i could use that pay to buy me a few real estate investments and some other things i know my girl wanna get married. "Hold the fuck up Ryder no way in hell are you and Cherry getting married before me and Destiny i would never hear the last of that. "Shit King maybe we can do a double marriage or something close to that after the bullshit is over." You know what Ryder that doesn't sound like a bad idea of course we gotta kill this nigga and all of his people that may become a problem later on but other than that im with it. " Well there it is then say no more King after this let's put that shit together. (ring,ring,ring,) Hello, Hey Ryder can i speak to King for a min, sure, is everything ok with y'all ? " Yeah we good, "Ok Hold on, aye king it's Destiny " Hello what's up baby? We were wondering if we could leave town on a mini vacation for a few weeks until things cool off ? " Look baby i don't know i will run it by Ryder and if we think we can come to you safely and get u out without compromising your safety then we will but look i gotta go i will text u or Ryder will, " Ok King later, (click) " What's good King? The girls are getting restless i think she was saying can they go on vacation until things cool off' "No way we moving them are we king you see what happen last time and even if we send guards with them they wont be here for us to look after them under our watch what we need to do is step this shit up and get these niggas." see that's why you my right hand we think alike say no more put the call in to the squad to be on stand by we bout to rush these niggas and slaughter everything moving. " Aye they ready King do we send them to the building the feds maybe still there," No we gonna wait until nightfall then my F.B.I. contact gonna tell us where his new location is then hopefully we end this shit now, she texted me and said they are at some dumping site where Killa is dumping a body and there maybe more they are getting ready to swarm on him and arrest him. "King we may need to put the word out to take him out i don't trust his bitch ass he may be a Killa but the way he flipped flopped back and forth between us and Just I'm not sure he won't run his mouth, "If i now Just and i do know Just, Ryder he won't live to even think about telling so let's just see how it plays out my contact will let me know everything and we will go from there. " You know what I agree King. (ring,ring,ring) "Just its Cole they about to get Killa at the dump site, "Ok thanks for the info let me know what they ask him and what the fuck he says how the fuck this happened. " Will they been watching and trying to catch up with you especially after the warehouse when you or when they thought you blew it up but i also think the guy you beefing with has some insiders on his team because they only want you so you know they will offer Killa the sweetest deal in life to get you but i can tell you he's no rat." Cole let me know what happens moving forward goodbye. "This stupid ass nigga gonna get his self jammed up i told his ass to watch your fucking surroundings at all time i bet he was on the phone with one of his bitches well it doesn't matter he has to die i can't take any chances but frist let me observe what happens then off with his fucking head.

CHAPTER 14: KILL OR BE KILLA B

Damn! I think I'm being followed shit i shouldn't have never came to this dumping site who the fuck is it the feds, King, or local police it could be anyone or maybe no one i could be paranoid that dam ups truck was behind me before then that yellow school bus fuck it whoever it is i ant going out like no sucker ass nigga i got my 45 with hollow point and my SKss all locked and loaded it's not goanna be easy but maybe I'm trippen i Dunno that dam King is sneaky as fuck dumb ass nigga really thought i would betray Just are you fucking serious just is the most crazy vengeful nigga on earth no way was i crossing him and the nigga King couldn't even give me a guarantee that he could kill Just but its cool i got my own plan wait it out until Just kills King or vice versa than i come in and kill whoever left and control everything (ha,ha,ha) stupid mu'fuckers think they can get me. But first let me dump this body and i won't use this site again about 21 bodies here and I'm getting paranoid thinking I'm getting followed let me back up and dump this nigga. (beep,beep,beep) what the fuck is a helicopter flying so low for, oh shit. Freeze mother fucker this is the FBI we have you surrounded turn off the fucking truck throw the keys out the window and i wish you would try a fucking thing and we will blow your fucking brains all over that dam truck. "Ok you got me I'm not moving dam Just gonna be pissed at me he told me be careful i knew i was fucking being followed and didn't take evasive actions i fucked up i don't know what these crackers got on me beside this fucking body in the bed of this truck but it's the feds dam let me shut the fuck up and see what's what. Ok mister Kamren Cook or should i say Killa B I'm agent Janet Davis of the FBI your under arrest for 20 counts of murder, 20 counts of drug distribution, 20 counts of intent to sell and deliver with a firearm 20 counts of conspiracy, and 20 counts of killing a police officer and before you say a word i came up with all the counts they equal to a hundred years and if your black ass ever want to see the light of day it's either you or your boy Just and i don't have a problem serving yo ass up if you don't cooperate oh and one more thing the federal prosecutor says anyone that don't corporate she's seeking the death penalty , so think about this while yo black ass is on your way to the federal detention center. (ring,ring,ring,) Speak!" they got Killa" Ok say no more (click) I need you to go find out if he's talking and if so if my name is mention can you do that, yeah i can even though the first day that bitch Davis kicked me off the case I'm still cool with certain people there and i still work there just not in her department the bitch really wanted me sent back to basic training. "If you would a did what the fuck i said you wouldn't have had these issues you do know FEDS were killed so of course she's on edge do what the fuck i tell you and don't fail me again. "Ok, I won't fail again. " I know you won't. " Ok Mr. Kamren Cook or should I call you Killa, which do you prefer? Call me Kam Mr. piece of shit FED officer. "Ok you a tough guy i see i will be right back and then we will see how tough you are. (knock, knock) Hey Killa I'm a friend of you know who he wanted me to let you know stay strong and he got you ok. "Tell our friend im solid don't worry about me be get me the fuck out even if he has to break me out. " I will relay the message ok got to go the officer is coming back. " OK Killa let me lay out what we have on you tough guy first the dead body you was dumping of the Kid Lil Spade well he has a family member in the pen called Half dead who was really in control and I'm sure you heard of him he waiting on you and your boss to hit the penal system also the other counts of murder, drugs, conspiracy and the countless other chargers on paper and in the public eye you where running everything, your boy Just set you up nice to take the fall on mostly everything while he looks like a fucking choir boy do yourself a favor corporate get a sweetheart deal we really want his lunatic ass anyway because if you don't at the least you will rot in a federal detention center if you survive Half Dead but you and i both know Just will probably kill you before then so Mr. Killa B what will you do. " Fuck you I'm no snitch and for coming at me like that the first chance i get I'm gonna break your fucking jaw bitch ass nigga. "Oh i see you one of those ok tell you what we will keep it off the record it won't be public knowledge like we do the rappers we won't say you bitch made and you can keep that gangsta image and if that's not incentive enough here is one for you your boy Just has connections in the department and from what i here they got evidence that you killed all them FEDS on the rooftop now what you got to say tough guy. "You lying piece of shit he would matter fact i don't know no Just do what the fuck you need to do i will never tell you shit and fuck a Half Dead that nigga don't run shit. "Ok Mr. Killa B after you spend some time in lock up getting you ass hole bent out of shape maybe you will reach out and change your mind good luck and by the way they found your mom dead this morning two shots in the head she was severely beaten and raped we not sure who did it was it King or was it your boy Just we figured you would know good luck on life take this scum to lockup. 'what homie what they got you on. 'Aye check this out I'm not speaking on my case, and don't ask me again. " Look homie. I don't want any problems. I know you plugged in with Just crew everyone on the cell block knows it i was making small talk. " I'm not with the small talk and I'm not ya homie and if you know who I'm with then you know I'm called Killa B and whether it's a gun or a blade I get busy so step off. "Ok you got that Killa. " Fucking mother fuckers i gotta watch out if one of these nigga try me i will kill they ass off period point blank i gotta get a phone call to Just. "Yo Killa here Just told me to give you these supplies. " Yo thanks fam what's ya handle. That's not important. I'm getting out today and I'm completing my promise to my people. "Ok cool. "Let's see soap ,toothpaste, toothbrush, phone card, some food, soda's sneakers, ah this what I'm talking bout a phone, let me put the homie up on what these mu'fuckers Tryna do. (ring, ring) Yo they got me and they all up in our shit I'm solid though so don't worry get me a top flight lawyer asap they talking crazy up here and they said someone offed moms have you heard anything about that." Yeah i just heard about that something about a junkie but I'm on it i got some homies looking out for you they don't wanna be seen but if you need trust and believe they are there." Aye Just you heard anything about some nigga named Half Dead pose to be lil Spade and Ace of Spades people they one really running the show the cops talking about he after us. "Yeah i know him i can't front he get busy but i got nigga on his head as we speak hopefully the off his ass but look check this out i already got word you staying solid so be easy we gone get you a lawyer and see what's what and if all else fails we break you out and send you to an island to relax i got you my nigga so don't think cause we at war with King the cops on my ass and half Dead want us dead we gone win this shit and killem all you'll see be easy son and hit me on the Jack whenever and don't worry if the guards or someone finds it, they won't be able to trace it back to me so on that note the lawyer should be out to see you soon and you got 10 stacks in your account . "Ok Just holla real soon. " Dam Killa is keeping it a buck too bad i may have to still kill his ass to be on the safe side i can't take no chances I'm gonna really have to think on this oh shit the phone not hung up hello! Killa you there. Dam guess he hung up (click) " that mother fucker after all we been thru and i told him about King's plan I'm glad i heard what his talking out loud dumbass was saying I'm no rat ass nigga but I'm gonna have to think and make my next move my best move but i gotta do this on the sly whatever it is i come up with because that nigga got eyes and ears everywhere dam just why u gotta fuck over even your own people I'm gonna wait before i take any action to see what if any move he gone make then i will act accordingly. " Aye Ryder they got old boy and from what i hear from the contacts we made in Just organization he still may Kill Em even though dude Tryna stand tall that nigga is a cold mu'fucker he kill off everyone even his people. "Aye King it may work in our favor his organization is gonna implode from the inside out watch what i tell you that mother fucker is gonna fall and when he does we gonna crush what's left of his shit fucking bitch ass nigga. " Yeah he will for sure Ryder but until then let's keep tabs on this shit and see how it plays out. " Well Mr. Kamren Cook did you have time to think over our offer of full immunity and we will give you a new name and up to 200,000 dollars and all we need you to do is put a nail in Just Coffin pun intended." I didn't even for once think about no shit like that I'm no rat and i don't know no fucking Just even if i did and even if he was to try and kill me i would never give up my morals on what i believe in." Ok you stupid mother fucker remember this opportunity you had when your doing life or even worse when you sitting in the gas chamber, guard take this low life piece of shit back to his cell. " Hey fuck nigga these cuffs to tight." Yeah i know i gotta make it look good for them people Just said take this phone throw the other one away or better yet sell it or give it away he needs to talk to you asap. "Oh yeah i bet he fucking do. "Calm down, he knows you are standing tall, call him you will be pleased . Here we are at your cell. " open cell block 9. Remember to call Just. (ring, ring,) " Yeah what's good Killa my friend ! "Stop the b.s. Just you gonna try and Kill me after all the shit we did and been through. " Killa calm down i'm not gonna lie i was but after hearing everything they threw at you and you still didn't fold you have no worries so don't sweat that shit it's business you know in our line of work you have to be sure one wrong mistake can end your life or freedom so my friend in good faith the lawyer is paid and he has some good news but i will let him tell you he should for sure be up there today stay strong and don't doubt my intentions we good it's all water under the bridge ok Killa you hear me. "Yeah i hear ya if you say that's what it is then it is I'm out I'll holla at you later Just. "One thing for sure if i get outta this or eleven if i don't when i meet up with his ass again he's dead bitch ass unloyal ass nigga but until then i will use his lawyers and what ever else to my advantage. " Kamren Cook you have a legal visit and get on the gate for the visit. " Dam guess Just wasn't bullshitting this time aye c.o. how long is the legal visit be for. It' however long your lawyer needs an inmate. Ok turn around so i can uncuff you but let me warn you if you attack this man or woman for any reason i will personally beat your ass until every bone in your body is silly putty you got that. "What the fuck you talking about why the hell would i do that shit. " you niggas always get mad when they can't get you out the b.s you done did on the street that's why, open door 4 now here go in and talk to your lawyer. "Hello Mr. Cook I was sent by Justin Clark, but let me be clear I work for you and I will never represent anyone that wants to snitch. "Shit loud and clear we on the same page I'm no rat never have never will be let's get to it what am i facing." you see that's it far as i see and after talking to the federal prosecutor and my inside contacts they only really got you on the body in the truck that you was dumping at the landfill now of course me and you know you guilty of most of the alleged indictment but I'm 95% sure your gonna walk on the truck and be free hell it may never get to trail you see here in my briefcase your boss supplied me with employee records and they say they rent the trucks from another company and they were filled up with dirt and debris already and you was dumbing it to start your concrete job so if i can get the jury to buy that and i will you will walk free and clear now with that said do you have any questions.,

ok none good i will see you in two days at the probable cause hearing and when you go back to the tier make sure you call Just and tell him thank you because without him getting me your black ass would see death row quicker than you think. "Ok i will hey what's your name again. 'It's David Esquire and tell all your lockup buddies about me. (ring, ring) Aye yo Just that lawyer was talking that good shit for real. "See i told you i got yo no worries my friend u will be out soon they case is weak they have nothing. "Good looking. Just i do feel reassured but you know how it is i won't be relaxed or feel at ease until I'm out of here. " I know my friend i know we need you back out here it's money to be made and that nigga King is slippery than a fish no one has seen him or his man Ryder i need you out here you always gets results but anyway let's talk later i got some business to handle. "Ok, I will holla another time. "Janet in my office now." Yes sir, is there an issue. "
Where are we on the Killa case? " Sir we are having some difficulties he, "Let me cut you off your case is fucked up Killa has a top flight fucking lawyer that probably will get him off all that shit and all we left with is a body in a dump truck in which he gonna claim he works for the company and never sees what's in the truck he just dumps them and all this ass hole needs is one fucking jury to believe him then he beats the fucking murder did i get all that right so far. "Yes sir you are but it doesn't mean he will beat the body i got the best prosecutor on the case." Enough of the bullshit you had the best prosecutor he called we spoke he won't fight a losing case and i won't either release Killa build a new case without the body and get him and Just and let me be clear Janet if you don't bring them down you may as well get you a Job at Mcdonalds or the state police because you will be done we clear. "Yes sir, very clear. "Good now get the fuck out my office. " Cook pack it up your case was dismissed. " Yeah that's what the fuck I'm talking about the nigga Just came through even after the nigga tried to have me merked, but fuck all that i got a new plan I'm taking shit over and getting rid of his hot ass all i gotta do is be patient and wait until the right time then off with his fucking head. (knock, knock) " Yeah who is that ? " Congrats you are finally getting released. " Yeah thanks but who the fuck is you nigga. " Oh me I'm nobody they call me Half Dead yeah by the way you look so shook i see you recognize me i was gonna let my crew do you dirty when i found out yo bitch ass had part in my nephew getting killed but then i got the call from King and we came to an understanding

so with the help of his top flight legal team i get out tomorrow. "
Mother fuck King and fuck you agggh. (thud,thump,swipe,swipe)
" Killa Yous a stupid ass nigga now see what you made me do your
all cut up and bleeding anyway before you interrupted by trying to
prove you tough i will see you and Just real soon have a nice day oh
by the way don't let the guards see you bleeding they won't release
yo bitch ass. (ring, ring) " i knew you would be calling your getting
released." yeah Just they just told me then right after that i go a
visit from some nigga called Half Dead. "Hold up Killa that nigga
got life you sure it was him. "Not only am i fucking sure it was him
the nigga stab me up not enough to stop me but enough to warn
me he's coming for us King David helped him give some time back
he's getting out tomorrow and he said to tell you he will see us
soon . " I'm not gonna lie Killa the nigga is a problem and he done
linked up with King but it's still fuckem I'm sending 20 goons to
pick you up from the Jail so don't sweat that shit we gone off that
bitch ass nigga to. " I'm ready Just to end all these niggas enough
is enough i gotta go they calling my name for release see you one
the outside. (click) " Fucking Just don't care i gotta get rid of this
nigga before he gets me killed i will figure this shit out on the
outside fuck, hey c.o. I'm ready I'm packed up. " Welcome the fuck
home Killa look i wanted to talk with you in case you feeling some
type of way about me putting a hit on you first of I'm Just mother
fucking Just in credible in case you forgot if i wanted you dead you
would be you know how this shit go but fuck all that i need you on
the team and not to have any doubt so as a gesture of good faith
I'm giving you two million dollars and more responsibility's i need
to know i can count on you so we can crush King's bitch ass and
cut Half dead's fucking head off his fucking body so what you say
you in or you out and if you out you still take the money but i don't
wanna see you again. "Just two mill damn son that's what's up i
appreciate the love fam and i did have some doubt but you put all
that at ease I'm all in. " Good to hear that lets end this shit once and
for all.

CHAPTER 15:
KING'S WRATH

Destiny i know it's been a lot for you and Cherry to be coupe up in the safe house but trust me it was all necessary me and Ryder got a master plan that's why we sending you two out the state on a private plane no one knows the pilot it's Ryder's cousin we need you out of here because we about to turn up the heat ,the city gonna flow with that nigga's blood. "Yeah you got that shit right King, Cherry i love you baby and i will see you soon this is the pilot my cousin Vaughn he will be your escort and pilot anything you need he got you here are three burner phones one for each of you use it if you have to, " Hello Ms. Cherry Ms. Destiny, I'm ready when you are Cuzzo. They are in good hands. King I will call soon as we touch down, "Ok Destiney i love you baby see you soon, "I love you too King and i can't wait. " Cherry you already know baby how i feel see you soon. "Ok Ryder you two get back safe to us we will talk to you later. " Dam Destiny, I miss them already and we have only been in the air for 2 hours. "Girl i know how you feel but the good thing is this b.s. Is almost over and done with." Ok ladies this is your captain speaking we are about to land in about 45 min Destiny, Cherry relax you're in good hands captain Vaughn at your service. " Hey King, I got the text for the meet up spot with Half Dead and told him we will be there in 20 min or less. "Cool let's be out and see what the play is to finally rid the city of Just." Pull over i believe that's King in the BMW oh yes that's him i see it's only him and Ryder you guys stay in the car we good here this brother word is bond. " Half Dead congrats on being set free this is my right-hand Ryder. "Thanks to you King my friend I'm free and ready for my team and you Ryder to murder Just ass in the most violent way possible. "So, Half Dead what's the plan my nigga and let me know if you need any weapons Ryder can get anything you need. " That's good to hear King i want this nigga to suffer for what he did to my nephew i got a line on some of his men now if you ready we can ride out right now but if you don't wanna personally get your hands dirty i get it i understand. " Let's go Half Dead I'm all in. "Ok let's load up. My van is pulling up now and I got 3 men in my car that will follow us. " Killa, did you get all the weapons ready? "Yeah Just we got the shipment and i gotta tell you those Mexicans came through with some new guns and some grade a heroin and coke, i gave the team the guns and drugs and told them to stay on point King, Ryder And Half Dead and their crews may try to hit us i kept some Glocks and ak's for us are you still heading out somewhere. "Yeah, you stay here until i get back i got to meet with the plug again to let him know this shipment was short then i will be right back stay tuned in the nigga Half Dead is slick. "Just I would feel better if I could go with these new people you got to join the team while I was locked up. I don't know them or their loyalty or if they are solid. " First thing never questions my judgement if i say they good they good second off i understand you and what you're saying but we need all the men we can afford Half Dead is the real fucking deal he has connections. "Yeah, Just he has so many connections his bitch ass couldn't get himself off look i understand you the boss it's your way I'm ready to roll out let's do this and end this b.s once and for all. "Ok then Killa I'm going across town I'm taken four bodyguards with me 20 will stay here there is another 50 I'm going to debrief on the situation, and they know you the second in command some know others have seen your face on the news so we good I'll holla at you in a few hours' Just cool. " Ok guys listen up I'm Killa for you that don't know me i don't tolerate disrespect or failure so if you don't get right what i send you to do then you may as well Kill yourself now because i will kill you and all you love if you fail any mission now let's get to it you all have pics you know how King his right hand Ryder and that fuck nigga Half Dead, look Just got, men with him and you ten are with me we first going to a few of King's blocks kill everything moving dealers civilians everything we wanna make things hot shut all his shit down force that nigga to come out the streets anyone have any questions. " Ok King here's the spot where they at i got men on the roof already and all around some of your men are here to thanks to you giving me access to your top hitters now me you and Ryder are going to the roof we got top notch listening devices planted so we can hear what they saying, Ok here is your ear piece King, here Ryder let's listen in Half Dead you got some top notch security shit i here them good they dumb asses planning on hitting my blocks killing innocent people yeah they gotta go Ryder you got that other shit in place.? "Yeah King i got men following Just right now they picked his trail up in the suburbs he got about ten men in 2 cars plus his car but we on his ass we got 50 Cal guns and rocket launchers on deck but they know not to kill Just, they gone take him to one of our safe spots and wait for you and Half Dead."Ok King you hearing this nigga and what he said you ready to give the word lets wipe these nigga off the map. "Let's go, hitem (boom, boom,) (blatt,blatt,blatt,) " Let's go down King most of them dead the Killa nigga still alive but hurt. "Oh, shit Killa watch out they on the roof they everywhere (boom, boom,) (blatt,blatt,blatt,) " Look at you Killa you're bleeding out you had a chance to be on the winning team but you was such a bitch ass nigga and scared of Just. (argh,) "King pleas homie don't kill me it's not what you think after Just was gonna try and have me killed i decided to play my part and act like i was with him but when the time came i was gonna slay his ass then this nigga here Half Dead came at me my mind was really made up, listen if you guys give me a chance I'm worth more alive than dead. " Fuck all the talk die like a man at least pretend to be a real nigga, but don't worry Killa I'm not gonna Kill you after all you didn't kill my nephew. " No you killed mine I'm not for the dying declaration you knew what it was in the jail , (click,boom,boom,) "Look at this thinking ass nigga now his thoughts everywhere stupid ass nigga fuckem then, King ,Dead i just got the text they hitting Just now so we need to go on to the safe spot they gonna bring em there. " One down one to go how you feel Half Dead." I feel fucking great but I'm gonna feel better when Just ass is no longer breathing im ready my men will take care of this shit and burn everything down let's be out the car is back out front.

CHAPTER 16:
JUST IN TIME

Just i think we are being followed and Killa won't respond to my text or calls. " Fuck all this shit Mad x, hand me my two macs they wanna follow. (boom,boom,boom, "Oh shit they took out the men following us oh shit Just get down. (boom.boom,boom,) " Ok mother fucker put the mac 10's down or die right here on the spot. " You niggas should know there's no bitch in my blood I'm fucking Just incredible, (clump,) " Dam son you came from the side and straight knocked his ass out. " Yeah,, he talk to fucking much wit the tough guy shit plus King and Half dead want the nigga alive, but fuck all that let's cuff this nigga and take him to these niggas. " Ok King, here's the spot let's all go in. " Dam Half Dead you got this shit set up right what the fuck is this a torture chamber." Aye Ryder i set up only the best shit to punish this hard headed nigga but me myself i rather just straight kill the nigga but we gonna see how far this nigga piss us off before we get tired speaking of the bitch ass nigga my men pulling up now with him. " What up boss this nigga was talking the most gangsta shit on the way over here so we had to fuck him up and gag his bitch ass. "Take the gag off Welcome Just it's been a long time i been chasing yo bitch ass but now that we all here you know Ryder, and of course you know Half Dead you murdered his nephew Lil Spade so you know already this been a long time coming so let's not pretend, your gonna die it's up to you if you die fast or a slow painful death. "King you know me spare me the speech fuck all you niggas straight like that. (smack,thud,) (drrr,drrr) "'Im Ryder but you know im the nigga you tried to kill his woman how does that drill fil in your knee caps." I love it can you drill some more you bitch ass nigga oh yeah i remember you i fuck Cherry that's Crazy Eddie's people yeah she likes it in the ass. (drrr,drrr,drrr,drrr) (argg,ow,shit,) " Dam that hurts so fucking good. "Let me try Ryder, " Hello bitch nigga im Half Dead i want to know where all the money and dope at most your people already dead and those who not has fell in line with us Killa is only a memory so to show you i did my research on you it don't matter if you tell me or not i have my guys hacking all your shit now so i will find out and i have your daughter on her way here, would you look at this King finally a reaction out his bitch ass, Ace pull his pants down let's see how tough he is when i castrate his ass. "Aye Half Dead fuck you (aghhh,aghhhh) that shit hurts fuck you your nephew died screaming like a bitch ha,ha,ha,ha,." King this nigga is tough, but his daughter is here so let's see how tough he is. "Dad who are these men what the fuck have they done to you. " Baby be strong. I love you but a coward dies a thousand deaths, and a soldier dies once if you kill her, Do it I'm at peace with my choices. (beep, beep) King it's her. "Hand me the phone Half Dead hold up for a man," Hello ok i see bye. "Kill this piece of shit and let's go, the Feds are 15 min away. (bang,bang,boom,boom) "Let's go burn it all the fuck down.(screech) "Slow down Ryder before you draw attention to us. "My bad King i was excited we finally got that bitch nigga now sky's the fucking limit. "King, Ryder that nigga must have been a thorn i n your side for a min but now he's past tense so let's look to the future. "Yeah, Half Dead us three gonna take over the whole fucking state and Ryder for your loyalty you are now an owner and boss nigga to "King, Half Dead good looking out but what's the plan. "Hold up Ryder we gone sit at the table we got your crews and other top niggas in the city and state here right there bang a left. " Let's begin this meeting you all have been brought here because your top in your city or region so you getting this courtesy, some of you know me I'm Half Dead most of you know King and Ryder, I'm speaking but make no mistake about it we three are one, we all are going to take over this state and all states around us King has all up north states since he's from Newark N.J. Ryder has all down south states and his base is Atlanta and all west and Midwest is mine . King take over the podium. " Look it's simple we got 100% pure coke, heroin and top shelf marijuana you buy from us don't cut any of the coke sell to your middle men as is the heroin you may put a 5 cut on it so that way you leave room for your guys to put another 5 on it so they can cake off if you follow these steps even your foot soldiers will be rich there will be no wars without permission. (fuck you) "who said that don't be a bitch nigga stand up, who are you? I'm Big Taz from Cali and I run with the cartel. I run the valley' Hold up Taz the cartel in your region and all regions are on board with us and we are aware of the different cartels in each area. We have an agreement to get the work from them. "No, you hold up nigga you're not my King and anybody in this room that let you pull this shit is crazy. " Ok Big Taz you gonna be the example Rodriguez please come from the back." Hello Taz, you do get your work from us, but this is like King say it is, now I'm done talking." Ok lil Taz i mean Big Taz, you heard it from your source get down or lay down. (fuck you) (boom,boom,boom,) " Now look and Big Taz he's now headless Taz. "Now the rest of you get in line or get lined up you have your instructions now leave our presence but remember this everyone will be millionaires if you do it our way. " King, Ryder, we are about to take this shit to a new level and hope you are ready to become billionaires. " I should change my name to Richie Rich instead of Ryder, "Very funny "oh shit Ryder call the girls tellem the G5 jet,s on the way to pickem up. Maybe we can take a much needed break, Half Dead, one more thing. "Yes King. " I appreciate your help on this matter, and I look forward to staying in the shadows and us three controlling damn near the world. "Say no more King, I agree

CHAPTER 17: MONEY MAKING MACHINE

King oh my goodness thank you so much baby you have been spending these past 6 months with me every day since you and Ryder flew me and Cherry back and you been spoiling me with gifts every day and i know Ryder has been doing the same so on that note go handle your business i won't be mad i understand it's how we live and plus you not in the streets like that your behind the scene in the shadows. " Ok babe i will see you later tonight i love you." Love you too. " Aye Ryder, how are things with Cherry? She understands we are the money-making machine and we let our crews and managers handle the day-to-day street shit unless things get hectic, or a beef comes right. " Yeah, we good King I think Destiny had a talk with her. " Ok good the pickups should be done by now so we can go grab the money i would put a lil nigga in charge of that but in this game i only trust a nigga as far as i can see em. " Aye King, you don't have to tell me I know what you mean homie. "On that note let's go check on Half Dead he hit me yesterday asking was there anything more achieving than being at the top of the food chain i told that nigga only thing can top that was being on top of the world aye pull over right here in front of the green house. (knock, knock) King welcome Ryder welcome i trust u wasn't followed. You haven't anything to worry about. My men were in two cars back making sure no police, no enemies so what's a good brother. " Well as you know since we've taking over and being killing anything that don't comply my people tell me the feds are lurking now don't get me wrong i know you got a source and you told me that bitch nigga Just may he rest in piss had brought the heat to the city with his bullshit but my sources tell me that this will be a full court press so with that said im going off grid you and Ryder know how to reach me if need be but no worries everything is like we said if any of us top three ever get pinched everything still goes on the money is divided as the same and we hire the best lawyers and by any means even if it's escape not one of us ever spends they life locked away Ryder, King, your thoughts, "As for me i agree on what you just said Halfdead (beep, beep) Ryder your thoughts , "Shitt you know i agree I'm just grateful you two put me at the table to be a boss and make boss moves what's up King is something wrong? "I just got a text on my pager the feds are close let's be out see, you guys thought the pager was to outdate this shit works for me, and it keeps me off them phones but fuck all that let's go. " King, Ryder come with me i got a secret tunnel under here that will take me to my helicopter, and we can be out before these motherfuckers know what hitem King warn your source not to come near this shit set to blow the fuck up. "Ok good looking let's go. " Agent Davis we have a location on the suspects as you know we really don't have anything on them they don't talk on the phones much and when they do it's all bullshit so we need to catch them in the act i want Ryder, Half Dead and King fucking buried in a cell underground in Colorado ADX or fucking Dead to you hear me? "Yes, captain loud and clear my team is two min out they're gonna keep me posted on what happens. "Keep you posted why the fuck you didn't go with them out there you're the fucking Agent in charge. "I know Cap but I'm following some other leads that are impossible to ignore. "Ok Davis whatever it's your case but keep me posted im leaving for today. " Ok Cap. " Half Dead thanks for the lift we will get up with you next week i will send the location to one of my spots." Ok King, Ryder be easy. " Hey Ryder, my source wants to meet up and take me to little Havana you know where but don't get out. "She is paranoid as hell King, but you know what I get it she police and a FED at that we need her in our pocket so i don't need to know her and for sure Half Dead don't by the way how you feel about things you trust him. "Yeah, so far i do plus his word is good not like that bitch as nigga Just was. "Yeah, I hear that but i got my people keeping an eye on him." Ryder look your my right hand so I expect no less. I knew you would do that anyway. " Ok King, where're here i will pull over by the entrance while you talk to your source. " Davis what's up? "King my boss is big mad we didn't get you or at least Ryder but i gotta be honest with you we probably gonna get your boy Half my deal is only with you and your team but really mostly you. " I know Davis, do what you feel. I won't interfere but at the same time he is a good dude so long as he is good with me I'm good with him. " King I'm glad you said that i want you to hear something we got on tape your boy Half does a good job at security but the source he has was busted by us and he's a undercover agent at that he took out a little insurance policy and record a convo with a mini mike here play this with your boy Ryder which by the way i did as you said and bug some of his shit he don't check he is good for you the guy is fucking loyal told his girl the only thing before her is you period. " I knew Ryder would check out and I hand picked him myself so what's on the tape? " I won't just listen then text me what to do. "Ok cool give me 20 min then i will hit you back." Aye Ryder let's go. She told me to play this disk then get back at her so let's put this in and listen. (So let me get this straight Half Dead you are acting like you are with King but the next time you get him at one of your spots. killem " Look officer I'm telling you we killing Ryder soon as i leave the next meet with theme then King i don't know how the fuck they didn't check my resume i kill all competition and i don't do partners and after that his whole fucking team will fall in place or die you see what King doesn't know is his bitch us to be my bitch and soon as i came home she let me cum all in her mouth so she with the takeover so as you see the King will fall and I'm getting him at his own house tanks to our bitch, ha,ha,ha,ha,) " King what the fuck do you believe this shit i mean I'm not surprised about Tryna takeover nigga do that in the street you can't trust these outside niggas but Destiny i don't know. "Ryder i been checked her out she was his girl before and to keep it 100 i notice something one day on her phone she had a name pop up that said HD i ask her about it she said she put one of her old high school friend name under it but to keep it a buck i called and he answered that's when i came up with a plan to get him out and get close to get all his contacts but i said if the nigga play the straight path i won't killem but you know Destiny was all the way in with me until she found out there was a way he could get out so i guess her love for me had limits now Ryder drive to the spot so i can kill this bitch myself. " Dam King, I'm with you. "Let me see your phone so I can tell my source to handle Half Dead.

CHAPTER 18: BETRAYED

King, I didn't know you and Ryder was coming by. (slap) hand me the phone bitch, what you slap me for? (slap) The phone whore. "Ok ok. Ryder King what the fuck is going on? "Cherry be quiet come stand by me while King handles this no talking. Ok Ryder. "Bitch did you think you could play me? "King you never hit Mr. before what the fuck is this about? "Half Dead and no need to lie I had my police bug your shit you two thought you would kill me take my money and sail off into the sunset now go ahead try to explain. "King baby I was playing him. I was gonna (slap,slap,slap,) enough of your lies all we need to know is if you knew about this after the fact Cherry. "Now King i don't know who the fuck no Half Dead is Ryder dont really tell me shit and i find it hard to believe Destiny would do this why would she fuck with her ex. " Did you hear that shit Ryder? " Loud and clear King," Cherry there no way you knew about this from the beginning because you didn't know her so when did she turn you and don't lie because like you said i never mentioned him to you so the only way you knew it was her ex was by her talking to you which she should have now explain. "Ok Ryder baby listen he came by they been fucking i had no choice and i felt like. "Enough I have heard enough you ready to bounce King, Yeah, the cleanup team is on the way so we can't burn the place down because he will be alerted. She tryna run King. (bang,bang) Let me make sure this traitor is dead for sure (bang,bang,bang,bang,) "Oh my goodness King you didn't have to do her like that please Ryder talk to me. "It's too late for talking bitch. (help, someone help, pleas) " Die bitch (boom,boom,boom) "Dam Ryder that fucking gun is a cannon took her head off. " Yeah, King a desert eagle 50 caliber will do that but fuck all that the cleanup team is pulling up they will wipe all this shit down and disappear the bodies lets go and we can throw the guns away in the ocean i don't trust no one with murder weapons." Ok Ryder let's go get the Jag truck. " Ryder dam king if Destiny was gonna let that nigga off you and Cherry knew my nigga, we was slippen and we can't allow that to happen again. "You're right I'm never trusting no bitch again that's for sure. "I second that King so what's the play now. "Set up a meet with the nigga before he starts wondering why the bitch dint answer the clean-up crew putting Senors and bugging the house and setting it so it will blow if the nigga go there first but remember Ryder he is not planning the setup until the next meet so we gone get his ass at this meeting that's why we getting him on our turf so we can handle his ass smoothly then after that me and you running our shit and his shit nothing will change it will be just us two at the top me first and you second in command but we are still one you cool with that." Hell, yeah King let's go ready the troops." Everything ok Dead? " Yeah i was Tryna go fuck my bitch Destiny in King's bed again and let her know it's almost time but she not answering maybe she shopping or something anyway the fuck nigga text me we gonna meet in Opa-locka so you and two other soldiers come with me i i will listen to this nigga that's on borrowed time and then the next meet take Ryder out i will get King at the house when he in bed and then we running everything. "I hear you boss but you don't think he suspects anything do you or what about Destiny can you trust her." Listen here, Goon I never took our organization in the wrong direction not even when i was in prison so don't question me now let that be the first and the last time you do. "Ok dead my bad it won't happen again. " I know it won't lil nigga or you won't live long now get the fuck out my face bitch ass nigga. (ring,ring,ring) " Aye what's up? If your offer is on the table, I'm wit it this nigga is crazy i been telling him not to do it this way not to, but he just called me a bitch ass nigga and im gonna prove I'm not so I'm in. " Say no more then see, you soon. (click) " Everything good King? " Yeah, just another piece on the chess board came into place. The meet is set, let's go end this. " he's pulling up now King and he got Goon with him you sure we can trust that nigga? "I'm 100 percent sure Ryder i looked in his soul and saw he was willing plus he knows i will kill everything he loves if he even tries to betray us but no worries i know if he snake his man he will snake us also somewhere down the line so when this is done you make sure he is done.

CHAPTER 19: WINNERS AND LOSERS

Ok King, what's so important you had to see me at your warehouse? " Well, it's like this Half Dead your bitch is dead there is no more Destiny you two bitch ass niggas won't be sailing off into the sunset. "King what the fuck you talking about. (smack) Shut the fuck up nigga before you get more than a slap it's over you had to be greedy matter fact before you die, Goon relieve him of his weapon. " Sure, thing King let me get that 45 from you Dead mother fucker (clump,clump,clump,) "Fuck you betray me and hit me with the pistol for.? " I don't answer to you no more niggas remember you tough you said i was a bitch ass nigga well this bitch ass nigga taking over your territory and King has given me the third seat under Ryder. " King, may I speak please.? Look at this nigga Ryder now he saying please go ahead speak you bitch as nigga. " Yeah King, I loved Destiny, she loved me we knew you would go crazy if we told you the truth. "Enough you bitch ass nigga you underestimated my power and my Gangsta and for that mistake you will pay with your life, Ryder give me your gun. "Here King it's already loaded, and the safety is off. " Now before you die Half Dead let me tell you something, you are not the only traitor here, my right-hand man plans on killing me when I walk out the door. "Wait what King hold up I would never (blam,blam,blam,) " Goon watch what i do to those who betray me. "You see Half Dead i got a couple federal agents on my payroll so i always have the people that work for me check out and bugged you see Ryder here figured when the perfect opportunity came he would be King of my empire and kill me his fatal flaw was he trusted his bitch not knowing she was double dipping and planned on betraying him with my bitch and you but of course you knew this hold up Half Dead my right hand is still bleeding (blam,blam,blam) " Now Goon handle this bitch ass nigga for treating you like trash. " Wait Goon, I'm sorry. (boom,boom,boom) "You right you are sorry look King my 50 Cal desert eagle took his head off. " Good Job Goon we gotta go my contact said the feds is 15 min out get the phone off of Half Dead matter fact just die like him (blam,blam,blam,blam,) " You stupid mother fucker you betrayed your boss i could never trust you i couldn't even trust my right hand but fuck all that now i will run my empire from the shadows and i will take over every fucking thing because I AM KING. (boom)" Dam what a fucking blood bath agent Davis we got Half Dead his right hand man Goon and King's right hand man Ryder all Dead and at the house King's woman and Ryders woman Dead and all Half Dead men dead but no King not a trace and to be honest we don't have anything on him, we don't know if he even dead or alive what should we do Ms. Davis. " First off, it's agent Davis to you second call off the hunt for King he not our problem we got the people we wanted although the Dead and i suspect Ryder got Killed in a shootout or something with these two Dead motherfuckers and while you doing all that i need to make a call. "Ok Boss I mean Agent Davis I'm on it. (ring, ring,) " Yes, it's done the manhunt is off. "Ok i will be in contact with you in 6 months. There is a new burner phone in your glove box, burn that one and Davis your 5 million is at the location you wanted it at. (click) Hello dam he hung up.   (TO BE CONTINUED)

THE END

EPILOGUE

2 years after getting away from the FEDs and killing all his enemies David King thought living in Brazil was gonna be peaceful but little did he know soon there would be a cartel after him and his loved ones and they didn't want peace all they wanted was death and control of his Kingdom.

ACKNOWLEDGEMENT

Thanks to my sisters Lalia and Mecca for showing me the way
i saw how you started your dreams and it inspired me to finally
write and get my dream of writing out to the world

ABOUT THE AUTHOR

Bobby Montague

I have been writing short stories and poems as long as i can remember i think i was around 7 years old when i wrote my first poem and since then i read every book i could get my hands on my goal is to grow better each time as a writer.

BOOKS BY THIS AUTHOR

King David

David King has been set up by unkown enemies and giving over 20 years in the FEDs but he vows revenge and will soon be released on appeal will he kill all those who betrayed hime or will he die trying.

King David Part 2

David KIng thought after escaping he would live life in peace but there is a cartel from Mexico that wants him and everyone he loves dead will this be the end of his Kingdom

Printed in Great Britain
by Amazon

41117232R00076